THE RIVER LOOKS AFTER ITS OWN

A young girl struggles to free herself from the malevolent presence of the river in this time-slip genealogical mystery

Leona J Thomas

Copyright © 2023 Leona J Thomas

This is a work of fiction. Names, characters, places and incidents are either the products of the author's imagination or are used fictitiously. Any resemblance to actual persons, living or dead, events or locales is purely coincidental.

All rights reserved. No part of this book may be reproduced or used in any manner without written permission of the copyright owner except for the use of quotations in a book review.

Cover design from an original photograph by the author.
Copyright © Leona J Thomas

For all the people who enjoyed the first book in the series, and especially Carol and Vera who pestered me to write the sequel - well, here you are!

And of course, for Steve and Daisy the cat.

CONTENTS

Title Page
Copyright
Dedication
Sue's family tree for Kate Laura Innes
ANTIQUE WRITING SLOPES
PROLOGUE

CHAPTER ONE	1
CHAPTER TWO	5
CHAPTER THREE	7
CHAPTER FOUR	10
CHAPTER FIVE	12
CHAPTER SIX	14
CHAPTER SEVEN	19
CHAPTER EIGHT	22
CHAPTER NINE	28
CHAPTER TEN	32
CHAPTER ELEVEN	39
CHAPTER TWELVE	45
CHAPTER THIRTEEN	54
CHAPTER FOURTEEN	60
CHAPTER FIFTEEN	63
CHAPTER SIXTEEN	68
CHAPTER SEVENTEEN	72
CHAPTER EIGHTEEN	75

CHAPTER NINETEEN	80
CHAPTER TWENTY	84
CHAPTER TWENTY-ONE	89
CHAPTER TWENTY-TWO	96
CHAPTER TWENTY-THREE	99
CHAPTER TWENTY-FOUR	104
CHAPTER TWENTY-FIVE	111
CHAPTER TWENTY-SIX	114
CHAPTER TWENTY-SEVEN	117
CHAPTER TWENTY-EIGHT	121
CHAPTER TWENTY-NINE	129
CHAPTER THIRTY	131
CHAPTER THIRTY-ONE	137
CHAPTER THIRTY-TWO	140
CHAPTER THIRTY-THREE	145
CHAPTER THIRTY-FOUR	151
CHAPTER THIRTY-FIVE	153
CHAPTER THIRTY-SIX	156
CHAPTER THIRTY-SEVEN	162
CHAPTER THIRTY-EIGHT	165
CHAPTER THIRTY-NINE	173
CHAPTER FORTY	176
CHAPTER FORTY-ONE	179
CHAPTER FORTY-TWO	180
CHAPTER FORTY-THREE	184
CHAPTER FORTY-FOUR	187
CHAPTER FORTY-FIVE	190
CHAPTER FORTY-SIX	194

CHAPTER FORTY-SEVEN	199
CHAPTER FORTY-EIGHT	204
Author's Note	207
Acknowledgements	209
Books By This Author	211

SUE'S FAMILY TREE FOR KATE LAURA INNES

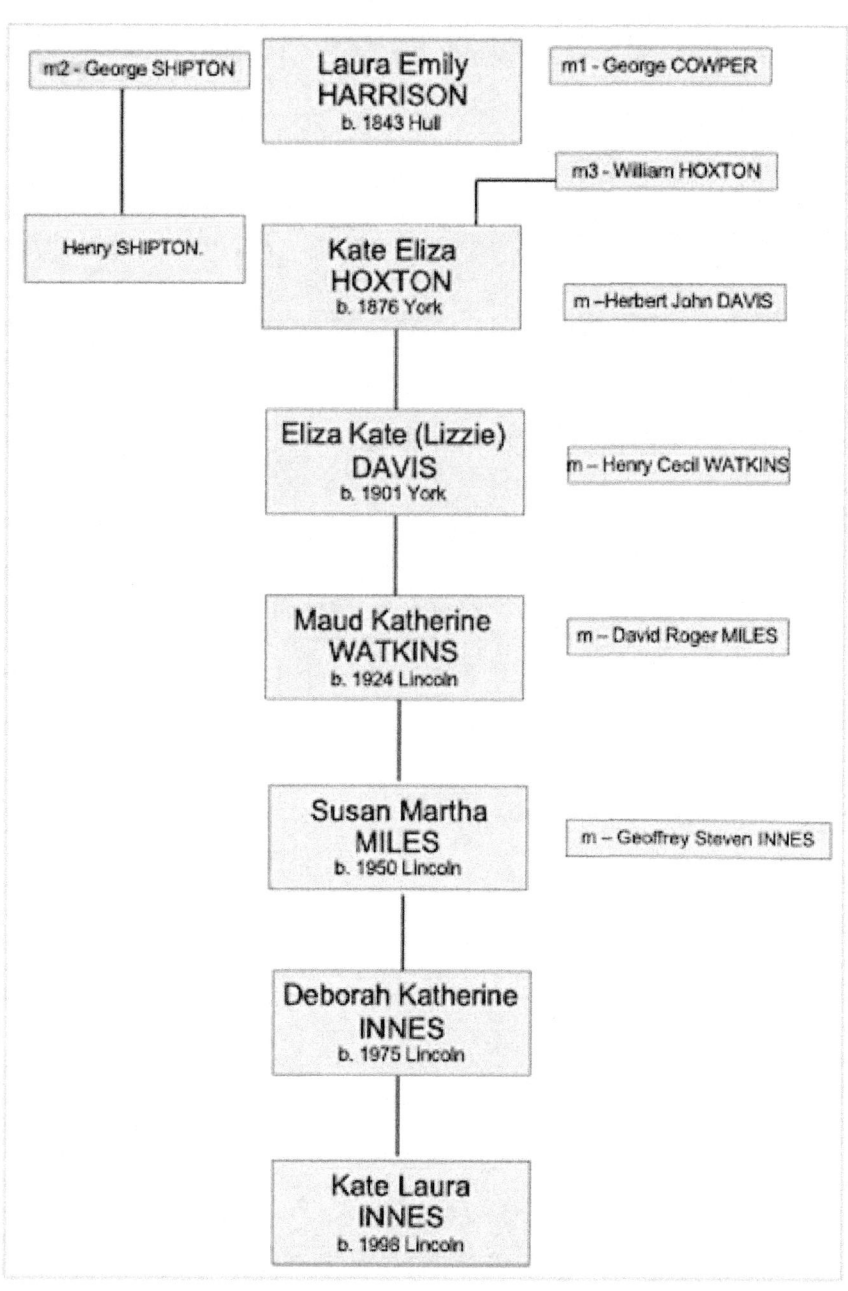

ANTIQUE WRITING SLOPES

For those of you unfamiliar with the antique writing slopes used in the past, this is an image of my one which was the inspiration for its inclusion in this novel. And the little cockle shell at the bottom right has a significance all of its own - as you will find out if you read on ...

PROLOGUE

1940 Cranfield Cottage, Skelthorpe, Near Lincoln

An overwhelming memory of black. That was how she recalled those times. Black crepe draped over mirrors and pictures. Black dresses, swathes of black net around bonnets, black armbands and sombre faces, subdued voices and those looks at her under hooded eyes that darted elsewhere when she met their stare.

She shuddered involuntarily as the memories ebbed and flowed through her consciousness. She could barely open her eyes now, the lids feeling weighed down as if by imaginary coins. She had no wish to open them, weighted down or not, on the other side and meet the accusing stares of those she had wronged.

The room was in almost total darkness to maintain the blackout regulations. Thick curtains were drawn over the windows. The only light a muted sliver that stole through a gap at the side where the dark fabric didn't quite reach far enough to exclude the grey dawn.

A door opened and closed, the merest disturbance of air like a cool finger that tried to invade the over-warm and stuffy bedchamber. The fire embers had long lost their glow. Perhaps no one felt it worth re-stoking the fire, assuming she would not last much longer. Economy – she would have approved. After all there was a war on…

In many ways she was ready to go. In others, she felt she had so much to say, to explain, to admit, to deny, to ask forgiveness for, to mitigate the blame they laid on her, albeit under their breath, from that fateful day – and maybe on other occasions?

Her mouth was dry, her lips felt dusty and cracked so that even if she could talk, who would make out the words? Moisture built up in the corner of her eye and a bead formed, threatening to overspill but she made the effort to turn her head so that it could not escape. She would not give the bystander the pleasure of seeing her weaken at the last hour.

CHAPTER ONE

June 2018, York

Kate slung a few rolled up T-shirts into the already stuffed suitcase and gazed forlornly at the heap of other items on the bed, strewn on the floor and balanced on the surface of every piece of furniture in the room she had inhabited while at Uni in York. She shared the flat with Jen, whose parents let it out as an Airbnb and, having let the girls use it in term time, had already had bookings for the summer season. Hence the need to pack up all her belongings, books, study folders and clear the bathroom of all her personal toiletries. Jen was in the other bedroom, applying herself to a similar task. Kate could hear music blaring from Jen's choice of downloads on her phone.

Kate sat on a miniscule spare corner of the bed and looked out of the first-floor window across the courtyard and at the matching block of flats opposite. These modern buildings occupied the space where previously Victorian brick terraces of back-to-back houses had stood.

Such a lot had happened over this year. And not all of it related to her studies, which she was really enjoying. She had been able to nurture her love of history and literature in a course that could have been made for her. But she had also discovered a lot about herself. And not all of it expected or even, welcomed. In fact, if she was honest with herself, some of what she had experienced had terrified her.

She had discovered another Kate – in fact, perhaps two other Kates; the second Kate, the one she never knew, or always knew – depending on how you looked at it – that other Kate, who had lain over her like a tissue paper layer, so thinly lain over her that at times she couldn't be sure which one was her and which was the other Kate.

She didn't know if this discovery was something that she was glad to find. No, she told herself – she felt more weary and uncomfortable when *that* Kate was around. If only Granny Sue hadn't started digging around the family tree and disturbing those roots that had sought the deep darkness to remain buried for all time. But of course, everyone was doing it now. Didn't everyone want to know where they came from, their family history and, maybe, the skeletons in their cupboards?

Kate's face broke into a gentle smile as she thought of Granny Sue and her arrival scheduled at any minute. All Kate's paraphernalia would have to be stashed into Cynthia, Sue's lime green Citroen 2CV, in preparation for the drive back to the only home Kate had ever known, as she had been brought up by her grandmother when her mother Debbie had died when Kate was only two years old. Jen's parents were arriving tomorrow morning and getting the flat ready for the first of the summer visitors who would be arriving that weekend. Then they'd take Jen and all her gear back with them. Kate hoped they could have the use of the flat for the next academic year. They were so lucky to have this accommodation compared to those who stayed in the students' residential blocks. Not that they weren't perfectly habitable, but Kate liked to get away sometimes and it was good to have this place to themselves.

Kate grabbed a hastily made sandwich consisting of two mismatched ends of loaves dug out of the nearly empty fridge, a dried-up slice of ham from a pack whose plastic edges were curling and whose 'use by' date was just past and a smear of some kind of pickle scraped from a jar ready to be consigned to the black rubbish bag balanced in the corner of the kitchen. As she snapped on the kettle, she caught a flash of lime green coming round the corner as Granny Sue headed for the flat's designated parking space. She hastily washed two mugs rescued from the drainer by the sink and considered whether her sandwich would stretch to being shared.

By the time she had added the tea bag to each mug, the doorbell rang and Kate opened the door to Granny Sue, resplendent in a multicoloured peasant skirt that flapped round her lower legs, topped with a lacy top covered with a casually flung scarf-cum-shawl. Her hair, now going grey, was pushed back from her eyes with a bandeau made from another folded scarf, the ends of which were tucked under her hair which almost reached her shoulders. Granny had never left behind being 'a child of the sixties' Kate mused, as she flung her arms round Sue and hugged her tight. Sue smacked a kiss on her granddaughter's forehead and announced, "I hope the kettle's on - I'm parched!"

"Lovely to see you too!" laughed Kate over her shoulder as she headed into the kitchen. Having refused half of Kate's rather sad looking sandwich, Sue assured her she had eaten an early breakfast before heading north from the cottage near Lincoln to beat the traffic. Hence her arrival slightly earlier than planned.

"I've not got too much more to pack," Kate said, mentally grimacing at her bending of the facts.

Jen appeared as she heard the voices, having switched off her music. Giving Sue a hug, she sat down and soon the girls were giving Sue all their news about the end of term events they'd taken part in, Jen being a little economical with the truth when it came to how late the parties had gone on for, or how she had felt the mornings after. Kate was more reserved than Jen when it came to letting her hair down, but she assured her grandmother that she had absolutely enjoyed the festivities, nevertheless. As Jen rolled her eyes at her, Kate hastily changed the subject, not wanting Jen to start telling Sue about one time in particular which had shaken Kate to the core. In fact, even now, she felt the cold shivers running down her spine. She made a point of collecting the used mugs and taking them through to the kitchen so that she could hold on tightly the work top to steady herself.

She had come face to face with – what? Who? She felt the colour drain from her face and was grateful to have something solid to hold onto as the chatter in the other room grew fainter for a few moments. Taking a deep breath, she felt her heart rate returned to normal and poured herself a glass of water, thankful that she would soon be back home and away from York and the dark mysteries it held for her.

CHAPTER TWO

December 1882, Naburn Lock, Near York

A woman and her child were drowned near Naburn Lock last week. Every effort was made to recover the bodies but in vain until Thursday last due to the extreme flood conditions when the child was found and taken out of the river at Acaster Malbis. An inquest was held at Naburn yesterday when a waterman gave evidence that the alarm was given when the child fell overboard. On asking the little daughter how her brother had fallen in, she said he tipped over after standing on the side and then her mother had jumped in to save him. This is doubly heart-breaking for the child as the boat was returning the body of Mr Hoxton, a well-known and respected waterman and coal merchant and the husband of the family, for burial in York after his passing in Hull the previous week. Verdict : 'Accidentally drowned.' The body of the mother has not yet been found.
<u>Yorkshire Gazette 15 Dec 1882</u>

They dragged the water for the next few days and eventually a small bundle, snagged in the dense undergrowth of the bank several miles downstream, was recovered and identified as my brother Henry. They thought I would cry when they told me.

The Shipton man and woman had come down from York the next morning to collect me from the lock keeper's cottage where I had been taken that night. They found me wrapped up in a blanket sitting on a stool by the fire with a cup of warm milk in my hand. They told me that my mother's previous husband had been their brother and brother-in-law but I really didn't care. I had never met them – or if I had, I didn't recall it. I just remember the scratchiness of the blanket and how sore my head was.

It seemed like nobody knew what to do with me that night. I had no other living relative with me. My father was in the coffin that the boat was carrying back to York for burial. He had died in Hull a few days before. Someone must have sent word upstream to York to the constabulary and they worked out who I was and who might be related to me. But they weren't. They said they had known about me but I didn't remember them.

My head hurt when they tried to get me to tell them what had happened. They said my mother had tried to save Henry. They said he must have slipped as the boat was buffeted by the swirling water. But I had my reasons – only I didn't understand them then.

But I didn't cry. In fact I didn't make a sound. I just rocked back and forth on that stool and clutched my hands around the cup of warm milk, listening in my head to what the voice had said...

CHAPTER THREE

December 1882, Leeds

The man held out his hand and the small girl took it as he led her up a path to the front door of an imposing house. All the lights were on in the front rooms and as they neared the door, it swung open cutting a streak of brightness through the gloom of the winter dusk. An older woman stood there, her hair covered with a white linen cap and a starched apron tied firmly around her fulsome girth. As the little girl mounted the three steps to the door, the woman bent, the better to greet her.

"Mrs Grimes, you remember Kate. Have you something warm in the kitchen that we might eat? The journey was tedious and this weather is bitter cold."

"Of course, of course Mr Atkinson!" Mrs Grimes replied as she bundled the child into the hallway, followed by the man, who removed his hat and shook off the rain spots that had settled there in the short distance between the hansom cab and the front door. As he did so, a door to the right of the hallway opened and a woman greeted them both, although she seemed unsure of what might be the best way to speak to the child.

"My dear Kate," she began hesitantly. "We are so glad to have you here. I hope you will soon feel at home here with us. You must be so …" but here she could not continue, instead raising a lace handkerchief to her face and emitting a small sob. "Your poor mother and brother…" she continued, her voice quavering.

"Now Eliza, come, come. This will not help. Get the child into the warm and let us rest a while."

The small girl lifted her eyes for the first time and looked up at the woman. In a tiny voice, more of a whisper, she replied, "Thank you, Aunt," and entered the room that the man had already stepped into. As she did so, her hand clutched at the small shell she had secreted in her pocket and as she did so, she felt a strength and comfort from it.

And so it was that little Kate, just six years old, came to live with Eliza, her mother's sister and her husband Charles.

*****

Over the next few days Kate began to become aware of the rhythm and routine of the household. She had been led up to the attic room which had been her cousins' nursery when they were young. A few of their toys lay in a box in the corner. A china-headed doll with a missing arm. A threadbare toy monkey. A pull-along wooden train. A battered cardboard box that contained a jigsaw depicting the countries of the world. But the item that drew Kate's attention most was a wooden dolls house, its door closed and dust lying along the eaves and paper slates of the roof. Aunt Eliza said she might play with anything she chose, especially as she had not brought anything of her own.

Uncle Charles had appeared early in the morning, two days after the accident. The Shipton people had sent word to Leeds once they were able to get information about her mother's relatives from one of the boatmen. She didn't know where the boat was now but she wished she could get her rag doll which she hugged to comfort her at night. Her uncle Charles swooped her up into his arms and said that he would take charge now, thanked them for looking after her and within a few minutes they were ensconced in a cab and heading to the station to catch the next train to Leeds.

But before they had left, Uncle Charles had talked in a low voice to the Shiptons and although Kate could not hear it all clearly, the words 'funeral' and 'inquest' reached her ears. She supposed that they must bury her father, as it was his coffin they had been bringing back to York, but she wondered about her half-brother Henry. And what about her mother? That was not supposed to have happened. At least, *it* hadn't said that it would. Yes, she thought, she would miss Henry. He was funny sometimes and made her laugh. He was – *had been* – two years older than her. But she had only done what *it* said, although she really didn't know why. Come to think of it, she really felt quite sad now. But she wouldn't cry. She decided that. She would keep *the secret* and no-one would ever know.

As Kate surveyed the jumble of leftover toys, her hand clenched around the shell in her pinafore pocket, the only item she had brought with her other than some clothes that one of the boatmen had brought in a bag from the boat to the Shiptons. It was a small white shell that had caught her eye as she stood by the lock at Naburn that dark night. It had been just at the toe of her boot when she looked down and she quickly picked it up and secreted it before she had been taken up the small jetty next to the lock and carried by one of the boatmen to the lock-keeper's cottage that dark December night. Later she might wonder why a seashell would lie by the bank of a river, thirty miles or more from the sea, but tonight it was simply a treasure to be picked up and kept.

CHAPTER FOUR

December 1882, York

Aunt Eliza was dressed in a black coat trimmed with a black fur collar. Her hat was swathed in black net and velvet ribbons, and her black leather gloves were tightly stretched across her knuckles as she stood clutching her hands together in the keen wind that blew flakes of snow across the cemetery. Standing by the graveside there were a few other people Kate didn't know and a few faces she vaguely recognised as people they knew in York. Maybe they were neighbours or tradesmen that her father had dealt with. The double funeral had been held that morning for her father, William Hoxton and her brother Henry Shipton, but of course, the women did not attend. But that afternoon they had made their way to the cemetery where they stood now, heads bowed, handkerchiefs clutched to red noses nipped by the cold, standing by the twin muddy mounds heaped side by side.

Quite a few people had come to pay their respects – and a few just to gawp, as was their wont. It had been quite an item of gossip and discussion. 'How dreadful,' they whispered, 'to lose them all that way.' 'A tragedy,' agreed others as they nodded in sympathy. 'I hear they haven't found the mother's body…' began another. 'Shhh…' they were hurriedly silenced as they saw Kate look up nearby.

Of course, she understood where her mother was. But she couldn't tell them. It was where *it* always took them. Sometimes they were found, but most times they weren't. She knew. She would always know. She didn't know *how* she knew; she just did.

Aunt Eliza stepped forward and laid a posy on the mound

nearest her. Then she gently nudged Kate and she stepped forward with her bedraggled posy and laid it on the other mound and hoped that it was her father's. She had loved him very much even though he was a lot older than many of her contemporaries' fathers. She loved to sit on the floor by him when he was reading the newspaper in their parlour and lean her head against his knee while watching the flames dance in the grate. But he hadn't been well for a while as the colder weather had come in and Mother was not pleased when he insisted on going with one of his boats down to Hull. The weather had turned after he left and a few days later they got a note to say that he was ill and they should come to come to Hull. Mother had hurriedly got some things together and soon, the three of them were on the train and in Hull by early that afternoon.

They had gone straight to the lodging house where her father often stayed, but their mother had entrusted them to the doctor's wife who looked after them that night. The next morning, she and Henry had been taken back to the lodging house where their mother met them and enveloped them in her arms. Breaking the news to them must have been hard for her mother, Kate thought later, but Kate had been brave and she didn't cry. Henry was two years older than her but he sniffled and she had been ashamed of him. The next thing she remembered they were on the boat with their father's coffin on board and heading through a fearful rainstorm back to York. And of course, then she had heard the whispered command. She did wonder why. But it had such a manner about it that you really had to obey. And Kate was always an obedient little girl…

CHAPTER FIVE

January 1883 Leeds

It had been a sombre Christmas for the family. The house had black crepe draped over mirrors and the curtains were drawn day and night. There had been a quieter than usual celebration on Christmas Day and the family had sat around the large dining table and bowed their heads before the meal as Uncle Charles gave thanks and then said a prayer for their missing loved ones. Kate joined in with the 'Amen' and looked across at her cousins Becky and Fred. Becky (Rebecca) was seventeen and quite grown up. She often looked at Kate with a sad expression and made to comfort her, but always seemed to hesitate when their eyes met. Instead she would bustle off to help Mama or fetch something she had left in the other room, or some other equally lame excuse. Fred (Frederick) was thirteen and he had been almost like an older brother to Henry on the occasions that the family had got together. He would show him his collection of lead soldiers and together they would have battles on the rug in his room after dinner. But Kate always felt alone. Becky was too old to play and Kate wasn't interested in the boys' games.

So Kate learned to listen. She sat quietly in the parlour when her mother and Aunt Eliza chattered. And she gleaned various interesting snippets of information. Like her grandmother had taken a turn when she had seen baby Kate for the first – well, the only time. Her mother had made the trip by train to Hornsea with her in the perambulator. From what Kate could make out, it was in response to a request from her grandmother.

"Laura, I do blame myself in some part for the result of that meeting. Mother has never been the same since, according to our brother Matthew. He says she has a weak heart and the doctor has prescribed rest and no more shocks."

"Well, it was you who encouraged me to go and see her in response to the begging letters she had sent you, don't forget."

"So what can have caused her to have taken such a turn? Do you know?" Eliza persisted.

At that, Laura seemed to be aware of Kate sitting on the little footstool in the corner trying to plait the hair of her rag doll, somewhat unsuccessfully it must be said. She gave Aunt Eliza a look that had them abruptly change the subject and soon they were discussing Becky and the family's plans for her. Kate stopped listening then...

*****

As the new year came in, Kate realised that her life would truly never be the same. She had to learn to accept that she would not return to her home in York, to her schoolmates and her friends, to everything she had ever known. Although she now lived in a busy house, with more servants than her mother and father had had, she still felt very alone. Sometimes she thought about running away. She could join one of the boat families and live a life on the river, never calling anywhere home other than the craft they dwelt in, worked from and travelled in. And of course, the river would be her constant companion then. She hadn't heard from it for a while now. How could she? She was always here.

CHAPTER SIX

August 2018, Near Lincoln

Kate couldn't believe she'd been luxuriating in the pool in Cyprus just a week ago and now here she was looking through a window covered with a haze of drizzly raindrops as the grey clouds swept across the fields opposite the cottage. Her golden tan was already beginning to fade, of that she was sure! In a couple of weeks she'd be packing up her gear ready to set off for Uni in York for the second year of her English Literature and History course.

It had been a glorious summer, spending time with friends, having long lie-ins, gossiping over coffees with friends in Costa and Starbucks, spending time with Granny Sue and best of all, not having any of those weird experiences that seemed to haunt her when she'd been in York. And thankfully, Granny Sue had taken a break from her family history sleuthing. Her evening classes didn't start again till the autumn and Kate was hoping she might actually give it a miss now that she had found out as much as she had. Certainly Kate had not brought the topic up and was hopeful that Gran would find a new project to focus on for the Autumn and Winter terms – say, learning conversational Japanese, or fusion glass picture making – even beginner's Tae Kwon Do, anything other than Genealogy. And yes, she could imagine Granny Sue taking any of those classes!

That's what she loved about her grandmother. She might be in her sixties but she hadn't given up on life one bit! Any new challenge invigorated her and nothing was going to cause her little grey cells to start to atrophy, not if she had anything to do with it. Okay, perhaps she was not as supple or full of puff as she had been a few years ago, but the spirit was willing even if the flesh was weak. Only the other week she had been pricing hot tubs with a thought of putting one in the small garden at the rear of the cottage. She had even drawn up a short list of friends she would invite to bring their cossies – and a BYOB of course! Even her fluorescent orange swimsuit was unearthed ready for the inaugural dip. But then the coldest, most miserable spell of weather blew in and none of her friends seemed to be ready to literally 'take the plunge' with her. Maybe next year...

As Kate pulled back from the window and pulled her sweatshirt tighter round her neck, she heard Granny Sue's voice calling her.

"Kate? Have you got a minute?"

"Yes – where are you?" Kate replied, aware that Gran's voice seemed rather distant and muffled.

"I'm up here – in the attic."

"Good grief! How did you get up there?" Kate remonstrated with her as she arrived at the top of the steep staircase and looked up from the landing. A small set of folding steps were sitting under the open hatch and from above Gran's face peered down, a few strands of hair escaping from a scarf wound round her head, reminiscent of a 1940's factory girl in a wartime poster. "And why?" Kate added.

"I was watching that programme – '*The Repair Shop*' is it? Where they repair and restore old family items? Well, I wondered if I still had anything of my grandparents'. This was their cottage too. Been living here for a few generations now. I'm not sure who was the first to live here."

Kate suppressed a groan as she looked up at the cobwebs gently floating above her grandmother's head in the draught from the open hatch.

"Is there a light up there?" Kate asked.

"No, but I brought a torch. Mind you it's not very bright. Think the battery's on the way out."

"I've got the light on my phone," Kate replied as she set her foot on the first step of the ladder, shivering involuntarily at the thought of brushing against the serenely floating cobwebs hanging from the rafters. Now she knew why Gran had worn a scarf.

There wasn't really room for the two of them in the cramped attic, set into the shallow roof of the cottage. Certainly the beams looked ancient and thankfully, still solid, if swathed in cobwebs and dust. Kate stood on the top step with her head poking through the hatch and reaching up, switched on her phone torch and swept it round the attic space. At first there seemed to be just a jumble of shapes and bundles, some leaning precariously against each other and none seeming to resemble anything in particular. As her eyes became more accustomed to the gloom and brightly illuminated spots of light from her torch, she started to recognise a few more familiar items. The artificial Christmas tree from her childhood. A box of wire hangers. An old, battered vinyl suitcase, its sides sagging in, showing its emptiness and lack of use. Bizarrely a pair of high leather boots – one lying on its side. Further in the items seemed harder to define. Most were covered in old horse blankets or piled so haphazardly together as to make no sense to the casual observer.

Gran bent over and shuffled further into the available space, taking care to place her feet where there were boards laid randomly across the old joists.

"Be careful Gran!" Kate warned. "When's the last time you were up here? Must be years ago from the look of it. What on earth are you looking for?"

"I don't know – but I'll know when I find it!" Gran smirked back at her, a smear of dust already across her forehead where she had swiped a spider's trail away.

They spent about half an hour rummaging about and finding nothing of interest. In fact, as Kate said, a good clear-out would be a better use of their time – and probably a bonfire at the end of it. Gran's response – "Philistine! You have no sense of adventure. You never know what we'll find."

"I think you'll find we have contracted asthma or some weird respiratory or fungal condition from the dust up here!" Kate flung back at her.

The sound of the clock striking five down below in the hall brought their rummaging to a halt.

"Gosh – that time already? I'm dying for a cuppa, aren't you?" wheezed Gran.

"Absolutely! Now for goodness' sake come down. And be careful!" Kate added, as Gran's knee knocked into a pile of cardboard boxes, knocking their contents to the floor. One fell apart as it made contact with the boards and in the dim light of the torch, Kate could see what looked like wood, a box, or something similar packed inside.

"Pass that to me, can you Gran?" Kate asked as she stretched forward to try to grab hold of the package. It had once been tied with string but that had frayed away and worked loose so that it took all her dexterity to keep the contents together as she tried to manoeuvre down the steps with no free hands to hold on with.

Laying it on the floor at the top of the stairs, Kate turned her attention to getting Gran out of the attic and down to *terra firma* before there were any more mishaps. By the time they both stood and took a good look at each other, they burst out laughing.

"What a sight!" hooted Granny Sue as she brushed Kate's hair back and removed a dead bluebottle from her shoulder.

"Well, you're no picture yourself!" laughed Kate as she snapped a quick selfie of the two of them looking like they had been hired as extras on a disaster movie film set.

"I'll put the kettle on. You have a wash and brush up and I'll see you downstairs," laughed Kate.

CHAPTER SEVEN

January 1883, Leeds

"We must look to getting you into school", announced Uncle Charles one evening, as they ate dinner in the dining room. The gaslights gave the room a cosy golden glow and illuminated the corners and flickered reflections danced off the paintings that hung from the picture rail around the room. Kate hadn't really enjoyed school much in York. She was a bit of a loner, although Henry always stuck up for her if any children started name-calling on the way back home. For some reason she never seemed to draw others to her. She was usually excluded from the skipping games or hopscotch in the playground. When a new pupil joined the class, the other girls would draw her aside, looking furtively over their shoulders, and whisper a warning. Kate didn't mind. She had another friend that she could occasionally visit if she went a detour on her way home or ran an errand for her mother. Not that Mother would have been pleased to hear about '*it*'. So Kate simply never mentioned '*it*'.

'It' liked to talk to her sometimes, not always though – and never if there was anyone else close by. Living as they did in Lowther Street in York, the river was the other side of the town. Her father sometimes took her down to the staithe when he would show her his boats being loaded prior to their journeys down the Ouse to Goole, Wakefield, Selby or Leeds. Mother insisted he keep a tight grip on her hand. He would tell her tales about trips he had done and sights he had seen as he used to man his boat downriver and back again. Nowadays he had some men who worked his flat-keeled boats for him and they did the heavy work now, but occasionally he would travel along to collect payments due or strike deals for future trade at the various destinations.

It was only when he was away and Mother was busy, that Kate could steal away and fabricate a reason for taking longer to come home from school or complete an errand. There had been a cart overturned and she'd stayed to watch it righted. A policeman had given chase to an urchin who had picked the pocket of a man at the market and the crowd had followed to watch the subsequent capture and arrest. A lady had stopped her and asked her how to get to a certain place and she had offered to show her the way. Her stories got more and more elaborate and there were times when her mother narrowed her eyes and scrutinised her face for any sign that she might be making up stories. But Kate could keep her face straight, a blank sheet with no lies scribbled upon it. Her clear grey eyes would lock her mother's matching pair and dare her to be the first to look away. She always did.

Henry saw her once. He was with some boys throwing stones, seeing who could get theirs nearest to the opposite bank. They were down at the Blue Bridge, beyond the park. She knew that Mother would be angry because she'd seen her fly at him when she'd found out once before. When Henry challenged her, Kate reminded him that if she got into trouble so would he. Did he want that? And so he was coerced into keeping quiet. After that, Kate never worried about him spotting her, if he ever did. But she preferred to find quiet spots to visit '*it*'. And there – sometimes – '*it*' would have whispered conversations with her. To an onlooker, it would simply look like a little girl talking to an imaginary friend. But of course, '*it*' wasn't.

And so now here was Uncle Charles talking of sending her to school. She missed '*it*'. She wondered if she would ever return and be reunited. It appeared that her new home was permanently to be with her aunt and uncle here in Leeds. And here is where her future appeared to lie. But to a six, nearly seven-year-old that seemed a very long way off.

CHAPTER EIGHT

August 2018, Near Lincoln

After a very welcome cup of tea, Kate and Granny Sue sat down to examine the battered and dusty carboard box that Gran had passed down from the attic. Kate could feel the grittiness of the cardboard's surface as years of dust had lain undisturbed upon it. The string gave way and soon fell to the floor at her feet under the coffee table.

"Maybe we should do this outside?" suggested Kate as she wiped her hands on her worn jeans.

"I think that's a good idea," her grandmother agreed and led the way through the small kitchen and out of the back door to the garden that stretched beyond the back of the cottage. Lines of beans under wigwams of canes stretched along the left-hand side from the small patio area towards a battered shed. On the opposite side they were matched by canes propping up sweet peas interspersed with pea pods, already fat and ready for picking. At the far end a small low bed held salad leaves, spring onions and shallots, while at the side of the shed was an area given over to hollyhocks and clematis using the rickey fence for support. Calendulas splashed orange and yellow faces beneath the taller plants and campanulas scrambled to cover the rest of the earth. At the very far end beyond the shed, a twisted and ancient apple tree bowed its branches under a crop of apples just turning colour and soon ready to be collected and turned into apple jelly, apple pies, apple preserve, apple sauce – in fact, into everything you could make with apples. Some would go in the freezer, some would be consumed and some would be sold at the annual village fête. The only patch of lawn was to the left of the uneven patio and across the garden was strung a sagging washing line which ended in a post set into the grass. A perfect cottage garden in fact and a tribute to Gran's green fingers.

A little rickety folding table sat on the patio by two garden chairs and it was on this that Kate laid the dusty crumbling box. There wasn't much of a clue to what lay inside other than an exposed corner from which could be seen wood making the angle or corner of a box of some description. Unsure where to begin, Kate turned the crumpled bundle around until she could ascertain where the cardboard lid had been folded inside itself to make a sort of tightly sealed top. It didn't take much effort to prise apart, the weakened cardboard giving up the fight fairly easily. Dust sprinkled onto the table and into the cracks of the crazy-paved patio and the cardboard surrendered, shreds coming apart and giving up the long-lost fight.

Dusting off her hands again, Kate explored with her fingers to find an edge to gain a hand hold and extract the mysterious 'treasure'. As she laid it on the table, brushing the remains of the cardboard box to the floor, Gran leant forward, her brows creased as she peered at the wooden shape. It was not a box as such. It had a flat top but the sides had an angled sloping cut which met the opposite sides. The top was plain wood but the side to the front had a small plate with a keyhole in it. It might have been brass but was now so discoloured as to be any kind of metal.

Kate sat back and slowly turned the box around. Apart from the key-plate, or escutcheon as Gran told her it was more correctly called, there was no other decoration. At the back opposite the side with the keyhole, a long hinge peeped from the join where the top met the back. At first they were mystified and then Gran drew in her breath and exclaimed, "I know what this is! It's a writing slope!"

"A what?" Kate asked, screwing up her face.

"I've seen one on *Flog It* or *Bargain Hunt*, or one of those programmes. People used them to write their letters on and inside there were usually compartments to hold pens and so on. Will it open Kate?"

Kate turned it around and crossed her fingers at Gran. "Let's hope it's not locked 'cos we don't have the key!" she chuckled. Gingerly she put her hands on either side of lid and gently attempted to prise it open. Initially it resisted, years of dirt and grime keeping the contents hidden for a final, few short moments. And then, with an almost inaudible sigh, the lid came up and Kate gently eased it open until it was vertical.

"Keep opening it, Kate. It should fold right back," Gran urged.

Kate continued till the lid folded back completely and lay flat upon the table. It formed a perfectly level slope upon which one could write one's correspondence. It had once had a handsome kind of leather covering, but that was now rubbed and shabby. A little worn loop of velvet was attached to edge of one of the flat boards that made up each of the flat surfaces. Kate gently tugged on it and the board gave a little shiver of anticipation. With a look at Gran, she pulled a little more firmly and it lifted up from its base.

They both leant forward to see what lay inside. The side which had the keyhole was subdivided into two, what appeared to be, wells for perhaps pens or other paraphernalia. Each had a flat wooden cover with a finger-sized hole in it. Inserting her index finger into the right hand one, Kate hooked up the lid but was disappointed to see that it was completely empty except for a ball of fluff. Repeating the same procedure with the left hand one, she was rewarded with a slightly better outcome. A rolled-up sheet of paper lay inside but when unfolded, was completely blank.

They both sat back, somewhat crestfallen at the outcome of their investigation.

"Well that was a bit of an anti-climax," Gran puffed. "Fancy a chocolate biscuit? I think we've earned it!"

*****

The box was consigned to the floor by the couch while Kate and Gran got themselves cleaned up. Kate was happy to throw her tee shirt and grubby jeans into the washing machine and ran upstairs to have a shower before dinner. She could still taste the dust in her throat and smell the mustiness clinging to her hair. Standing under the shower she just couldn't see the fascination people had for rummaging about amongst old junk. The television schedule was stuffed with programmes about finding bargains, collecting antiques, renovating junk into money-making items and the rest. Kate just couldn't see the pleasure people got from it. As far as she was concerned, much as she loved history and reading about it, grubbing about with dusty artefacts just wasn't her thing.

By the time she had dried her hair and thrown on a vest and pyjama bottoms, Gran had nearly finished making some pasta and the smell of ready-to-bake rolls heating in the oven had Kate's stomach grumbling with anticipation. Gran had changed into a pair of all-in-one dungarees with contrasting patch pockets. Her hair was loose and tied back with a bandeau of multi-coloured cotton. She looked fresh as a daisy and Kate couldn't help but marvel at her energy and get-up-and-go.

"Red wine or white?" asked Gran.

"What's the pasta?" asked Kate.

"Good old spag bol!' laughed Gran, "So red?"

"Suits me!" Kate chuckled, grabbing a couple of glasses from the kitchen cabinet above her head and taking them through to the lounge. Two chairs beside a small table with fold up leaves fitted neatly into the corner of the room and served them ideally as somewhere to eat, but could be easily folded out of the way afterwards to afford a little more space. The dimensions of the cottage did not translate well to the demands of modern living, but it suited them both perfectly and Kate couldn't imagine it any other way.

"Dinner is served!" called Gran and Kate turned to help bring through the food. A pang of sadness went through her as she realised that in a few weeks she'd be back in York at the flat with Jen and her second year at Uni would be starting. But for now she'd make the most of her time with Gran.

*****

"Ouch!" Kate gasped as she groped her way into the lounge later that night, having left her phone somewhere. It was only as she went to put it onto charge by her bed that she realised she must have left it downstairs. The lights were out but a soft luminosity bathed the room, the curtains were open and the late summer dusk with an almost full moon was enough to guide her through the familiar layout of the room. Sliding her hand between the seat cushions of the couch, she wriggled her fingers till they made contact with the hard rectangular form of her phone.

Turning round, she flopped onto the nearest cushion and rubbed her bruised toe, silently cursing whatever had been the cause. After a few moments, as the throbbing subsided, she considered what could have been the culprit. She knew the layout of the room like the back of her hand so she was momentarily puzzled. Leaning over the arm of the couch, she looked down and for a moment could see nothing which might have been the cause of her pain. She reached down and felt with her fingers until she felt a hard shape at the side of the couch. Temporarily baffled, it then became clear. It was the box, the writing slope they had brought down from the loft. She'd left it there earlier and she had no-one to blame but herself for her injury, as she should have moved it out of the way before going up to bed.

Muttering a few choice words under her breath, she stood and picked up the box, tucking it under her arm to head back up to her room where she dumped it on the floor, well out of the way of her bare toes till she could decide what to do with it in the clear light of day.

CHAPTER NINE

1883 Leeds

Sometimes Kate felt sad, and then she sat on the hard nursery bed and swung her legs and thought about Mother and Henry and Father. She hadn't realised that this would be the outcome. But '*it*' hadn't told her that, of course. She decided that '*it*' wasn't as much of a friend as it had seemed to be. After all, it wasn't anywhere near now. And she had lost everyone. What had it done to help? Nothing…

She decided if she ever met '*it*' again she would tell it that she didn't want to be friends anymore and that it should go away and stop talking to her. Friends were supposed to look after each other and be kind to each other. '*It*' wasn't a friend at all. So what was it? She thought really hard about that, but she couldn't come up with an answer.

When she felt like this, she curled up on her bed and felt under the pillow where she put the only thing she had which reminded her of that night. She had kept it because she thought maybe Henry might have seen some of them too when he was in the river. Did he speak to '*it*' too, she wondered. Her fingers curled around the white seashell. She didn't know what kind it was but she liked to run her fingers over the ridges and think it looked like a little, hard, curved fan sitting on the palm of her hand, almost but not quite covering it. People said you could hear the sound of the sea from a seashell but when she tried, she didn't hear anything. Well she wouldn't, would she, she reasoned. It was found beside the river, not the sea.

As the weeks and months passed, Kate attended her new school and gradually settled into the routine of the household. In the evenings she would be allowed to sit with the family in the drawing room. Sometimes Uncle Charles was there but often he was away on business and it was just Aunt Eliza doing her embroidery and Becky wistfully thinking about the new dress she had been promised for spring, and a new hat too. After all she was a young lady of seventeen now and about to mix with some of the society people of Leeds. Frederick, at nearly fifteen, was ready to join one of Uncle Charles' businesses as a trainee clerk, although Aunt Eliza made it clear this should be only a part of his training in order to follow his father into business and in time, he could work his way up to be a manager of one of his father's many business concerns.

Kate didn't pay much attention to their chatter. She was allowed to choose a book from the nursery bookcase to sit and read, or a wooden puzzle to play with. Her favourite, though, was the Noah's Ark, but it was too big to carry downstairs so she just brought a few of the pairs of animals and organised them. She liked to imagine the Ark on 'her' river. Father would be Mr Noah and Mother would be Mrs Noah. Henry could be Shem, or Ham, or Japheth – whichever one he'd like to be, and she would be... well, she didn't know but she thought she could maybe be someone hired to look after the animals. That wasn't in the Bible story, but she thought that there might have been someone anyway.

A knock at the drawing room door and the housekeeper, Mrs Grimes, came in with a tray of hot chocolate for the children and tea for Aunt Eliza and Becky. She was followed by the maid, Bridget, who carried a coal scuttle to replenish the fire as the evening was chilly for March. Bridget was 'a witless creature who seemed afraid of her own shadow' – Mrs Grimes' words to Aunt Eliza when Kate overheard them talking in the hall the other morning. She was clumsy and awkward, all the more nervous as now everyone's eyes turned to watch her unsteadily attempt to lay a few coals upon the dwindling fire. She dropped the small shovel, then, as she mumbled an apology, her eyes met Kate's. For a mere moment they were locked together, then she gasped, clutching at her apron, stepped backwards and just missed stumbling into Becky's lap.

"Be more careful, you stupid girl!" exclaimed Becky, hastily brushing imaginary coal smudges from her skirt. Aunt Eliza frowned at her daughter but said nothing as Mrs Grimes grasped Bridget's wrist and twisted her round and propelled her through the door. As she reached to close the door she turned and said, "I'm very sorry about that Madam. I have been trying to train the girl but I fear she's beyond hope."

"Thank you, Mrs Grimes. I will speak to you tomorrow," replied Aunt Eliza. Laying her embroidery in her lap, she turned to Becky and continued, "Becky – you do not need to speak to the staff in that manner." Holding up her hand to silence Becky's retort, she continued, "Even if the unfortunate girl is quite lacking in any grace or ability, you should not lower yourself in that manner. When in time you will be running your own household, I would advise you to consider how you treat your servants. You need to earn their respect and with that, their loyalty. Think about what I have said Becky."

"Well, she is a foolish Irish dolt," retorted Becky under her breath.

"Enough!" Aunt Eliza snapped, raising her voice for the first time that Kate had ever heard.

Meanwhile, Kate had a moment of vicarious pleasure as she sensed the latent power that she seemed to possess in just one glance. She had sensed it once before, when the oldest and bossiest of the girls at school had advanced upon her the first day she had attended. Just as the other girls grouped behind Bessie, Kate focussed her glare on the older girl's eyes and dared her to come any further. She didn't know how she did it, or even what she did, but Bessie jerked to a halt and burbled some words then backed away, gathering her entourage with her. After that, no-one bothered Kate – or bothered with Kate, and she spent many lonely times with her back against the school wall in the playground.

CHAPTER TEN

August 2018, Near Lincoln

Kate awoke to a grey morning and a misty drizzle in the air. It did not inspire her to leave the comfort of her bed but she could already hear Gran up and about. A light tap on her door was followed by Gran's voice. "Want a cuppa? I'm just going down."

"Thanks, I'll be down in a minute," Kate replied, stretching out under the light cover, enough for these summer nights, and then throwing it back as she turned to sit on the edge of the bed. Not much of a day for outside pursuits. She considered texting one of her mates and going into Lincoln to do some shopping. She'd see what Gran had planned first, she decided, and take it from there.

Throwing a cotton robe over her shoulders, she headed downstairs where the kettle was just boiling and the clatter of spoons and mugs could be heard from the kitchen. Gran stood by the work-top, hair scrunched into some semblance of a bun with the ends sticking out at all angles. She wore a silky kimono-styled robe, vibrant in shades of shocking pink, turquoise and emerald-green. Around her rounded middle it was fastened with a tasselled cord in a brilliantly mismatched shade of orange. 'Well if that sight didn't wake you up, nothing would!' Kate thought ruefully.

"Any plans for today?" Gran asked, briskly stirring the teabags around each of the mugs. Before Kate could answer, Gran continued, "Mrs Bailey from the WI – you remember her, don't you? Loves the sound of her own voice? Big hats? Volunteers at the library when they're short-staffed? Scares the kiddies in the playgroup?"

None of these seemed to fit anyone that Kate could recall, and seeing her puzzled expression Gran continued, "Doesn't matter... anyway she has asked me to come down and help her sort out the workshops for the coming term. Seems to think I'm a 'good organiser'."

Kate snorted and almost choked on her first sip of tea. Gran! An organiser?

"I know, I know!" laughed Gran, "but this way I can get a peek at what courses are coming up and maybe get first dibs!" she continued, adding a theatrical wink.

"Oh Gran! You are incorrigible!" Kate chuckled. "Any idea what the forecast is for today?"

"They said it'll carry on like this till early afternoon, then brighten up. Well, the garden needs the rain so let's look on the positive side. Have you any plans?"

"Not sure. I'll text a couple of mates and see who's up for some shopping in town."

"OK. Well I'd better get myself kitted out to impress Mrs Bailey then," winked Gran again, and headed upstairs, balancing her mug and a couple of biscuits on a small tray.

It was the kind of weather that didn't inspire you to do much and Kate couldn't summon up much enthusiasm for anything. Having slumped on the couch and watched a bit of the news and breakfast telly, she roused herself and headed upstairs. The bathroom was free so she decided a nice hot shower was in order. By the time she had collected a towel from the airing cupboard and shut the bathroom door, Gran was on the landing heading downstairs.

"See you later Kate! Have a good day. Let me know what time you'll be back if you go out."

"Will do, Gran. Have fun!" Kate shouted through the bathroom door as Gran's footsteps disappeared down the stairs, followed a few moments later by the front door closing.

Kate returned to her room a good twenty minutes later, smelling sweetly of jasmine and neroli, courtesy of a gifted shower gel left over from Christmas. She had exfoliated and oiled, massaged and moisturised until she felt calmer and more optimistic about the day ahead.

Sitting on the bed, wrapped up and oozing scented oils, her eye was caught by the box she had left in the corner the night before. In daylight it looked even sadder and scruffier. The corners were worn and the edges were uneven where it had suffered numerous bumps and scrapes throughout its life. But, she supposed, it had a sort of charm of its own. After all, it had survived all this time. And who had put it up in the attic? When? Why? Deciding she owed it a little TLC after being so dismissive about it last night, she resolved to have a better look at it downstairs in the cold light of day.

Having spread a few sheets of newspaper on the kitchen work-top and unearthed some old cloths from Gran's cleaning cupboard, she had a closer look at the box. First, she gave it an all-round wiping down. Then she sat back and had a good look at it. Well, nothing of interest really. It was plain, unadorned and without any form of carving or inlay. Just a plain wooden box. Or, more correctly, a writing slope as Gran had informed her. Who would have used such a thing? When? Her historical curiosity kicked in and much to her surprise she found herself intrigued to know more about it. Taking her phone from her back pocket, she Googled *'writing slope'* and sat back to look at the results.

The vast majority were for ones being offered for sale on auction sites like eBay so she flicked through the various images. Most, if not all, were far more ornate than the plain form in front of her. Then she altered the Google search to *'history of writing slopes'*. She discovered that they were made from a variety of woods, including mahogany, walnut and rosewood. Some had an inlay of patterns of a lighter coloured wood and the more ornate boxes had brass to protect the corners from damage. Half an hour later she had been drawn in to reading various articles about their appearance from mediaeval times right up to the Victorian era. References in Dickens and Austen had her hooked and she realised she had landed upon a topic which she found intriguing. Oh, if only her box had been a bit more elegant and prepossessing!

She sat back and looked a little more critically at the battered, shabby item on the table – a million miles away from the shiny, decorated and brass-bound beauties on screen. Opening it again, she ran her hand over the scuffed remnants of leather that stuck resolutely to the flat inner boards. She fiddled again with the lids of the two compartments under the front board and looking inside, sighed that they still held the ball of fluff and the crumpled sheet of blank paper respectively. The thought flitted through her head – 'this is the equivalent of today's laptop!'

Feeling somewhat ashamed of her initial, rather callous opinion of the box, she retrieved a can of furniture polish from the cupboard and set to, giving the box its first bit of care in – well, who knows how many years? Starting with the top, then the sides she sprayed and buffed, as the box begrudgingly began to attempt to shine, although the small brass shield on the top was so tarnished and rubbed that it made little difference. Finally she turned it over onto its top and set to work on the base. But as she did so, she thought she could hear a faint rattle from inside the box. Turning it back the right way, she heard nothing, but when she turned it back onto its top again, the sound could be heard a second time.

Puzzled, Kate righted the box and opened it up. She had checked the compartments twice now and apart from the fluff and paper, there was nothing which would have made that sound. Replacing the board, which lay sloping towards her and covering the compartments, she looked at the board further away. It didn't have a little shred of cloth to pull it up as the other one had and it appeared to be fixed. Kate fiddled around the edges but could see nothing out of the ordinary. Taking the polishing cloth, she ran it over the lower board, then the upper one to restore some of its former appearance. As she pulled the cloth over the side of the upper board, a thread from the duster snagged on something. As she reversed the direction of the sweep she had just done and unhooked the thread, she saw that there was a sliver of wood which sat snuggly along the right-hand edge of the board. As she pressed on it, it appeared to rock a little. Then she pressed on one end and the opposite end rose a little above the edge. She could just get some purchase with her nail and began to tease it up. As she did so she could see a little piece of wood about an inch long set at right angles inside. As she pushed against it, it started to turn and after she had turned it through ninety degrees, it released the top board and allowed it to hinge backwards.

Kate sat back and surveyed the box, amazed at her discovery. A secret compartment. She had read that many boxes did have such things to store love letters or important documents. What could be in this one? Her heart beat faster as her imagination ran away with her. Leaning forward, she peered into the space. It was empty and filled with the obligatory fluff and dust. But there was another compartment at the far side which also had a top with a hole in it, just big enough for a finger to be inserted to hook it open.

It was such a small space that at first, she didn't think that anything was inside but then she reached into the far end with her fingers and felt something soft, but firm. Working with her thumb and index fingernails, she managed to catch enough of the cloth so that she could extract the little bundle. It was a ball of off-white cotton, rolled around something.

Clearing a space, she laid it on the table beside her and gingerly turned it over to find where the material overlapped. It was quite a fine cotton and on closer inspection there appeared to be a frill of greying lace at one edge. After a few moments of careful dissection, it turned out to be a handkerchief. Inside it was a scrunch of tissue paper which held a harder item. First Kate smoothed out the handkerchief and had a closer look. Three corners were plain but the fourth corner had a triangular inset of lace to complete the shape. And there was an embroidered motif. It took a few minutes for Kate to decipher the intertwined stitching but it appeared to be two curlicue letters. One looked like an E and the other a K but they twisted through each other so that Kate couldn't be certain.

Turning her attention to the tissue paper bundle, even as she started peeling back the corners, it was crumbling and tearing in her fingers. In the end she had a shredded pile of grubby paper lying in front of her. As she searched through the last layer, her fingers touched something cool and solid. As she gripped the edge and flipped it onto the palm of her hand, she saw that it was a seashell, white and fan-shaped. She dredged her memory to identify it – summer holidays by the beach, collecting shells in a bucket. What were these ones called? That was it – a cockle shell. It lay on her hand, about half the size of her palm. The edges were crisp and sharply delineated, the narrow end rounded and smooth. She felt the sharp points digging into her hand as she curled her fingers tightly around it.

*****

She sat back on the narrow bed and looked across at the tall window where the dark drapes hung on either side. The rain ran down the panes, the centre one of the nine was a little misshapen and caused anything you looked at through it to be distorted. Not that Kate could see out of it unless she dragged the nursery chair over and stood on tiptoes upon it. She swung her legs back and forth, kicking the heels of her button boots against the metal bedstead, the thuds ringing out a muffled rhythm in the empty room.

CHAPTER ELEVEN

1887 Leeds

The day dawned bright, with just a hint of autumn in the air. As Kate looked from the window, she could see the first few leaves on the sycamore tree across the road beginning to tinge with gold. The summer had been a warm one, there had been less rain than usual and the rivers were low. In the last week there had been torrential rainstorms interspersed with bright sunshine, and the waterways were once more running full. Uncle Charles was able to get the goods required for his building projects on time and the duck pond in the park once more echoed to the calls of the waterfowl and the cries of children feeding them and sailing their little toy boats around the edge.

The Atkinson household had seen a flurry of excitement as Becky's engagement to the son of one of Uncle Charles' associates had been announced. Becky was quite the young lady now, and above sharing her time with Kate. She took great pleasure in flaunting her engagement ring, which she had received from Arthur Billings as a mark of his undying affection, while Mr Billings Senior flaunted the merging of two successful business families as a shrewd commercial opportunity, and the prospect of great expansion in both families' business empires as a result.

Kate pondered on whether she might be a bridesmaid at the coming nuptials to be held at the end of September, but soon was disappointed when Becky announced that her fiancé's sister Adelaide, as well as three of her own friends were to fill those positions. Kate would be relegated to a seat on the bride's side of the church and at the further end of the top table at the wedding breakfast to be held in Leeds Town Hall. Kate very quickly appreciated where she fitted in this family's regard. It wasn't that Aunt Eliza or Uncle Charles went out of their way to exclude her meaningfully, but she was always the outsider. She had attended school nearby and was always well-dressed and, as neighbours remarked behind their hands, 'a credit to the family'. She never caused a fuss, never had tantrums or made demands, never gave them cause to regret taking her in. But neither did she feel that she could share her thoughts or opinions with them.

She once overheard Aunt Eliza talking to a friend of hers in the drawing room when she was heard to say, "I never really know what the child is thinking. She keeps to herself. She is no bother, I must say, and we have never regretted taking her in."

"Such a charitable thing to do, I'm sure. A good Christian act. Such a terrible thing to have happened…"replied the other lady.

At that, Kate crossed the hallway and let herself into the kitchen where Mrs Grimes was taking the weight off her feet in a chair by the stove, while Bridget peeled potatoes and scraped carrots on the scrubbed kitchen table. Kate often would prefer to sit in the cosiness of the kitchen, rather than the gloomy nursery room where she still was accommodated. Perhaps she might get to stay in Becky's room once she was married, she found herself hoping.

"Ee, Missy, what can I get ee?" Mrs Grimes asked, looking up as Kate slipped through the door. She slipped into her Yorkshire dialect when she wasn't addressing the master and mistress, and Kate felt more comfortable when she did, reminding her of her own family, her lost family…

"Will you tell me about my mother again?" Kate asked.

"Ah'm sure I've telt it to ee so many times now, lass. What d'ye want t'know?"

"What did she look like? Just tell me again, please… It will soon be five years since I lost them and I want to remember her all my life. Aunt Eliza always gets so tearful and upset when I talk about my mother," begged Kate.

"Well, sit ee on't this 'ere chair 'side me. Bridget, get going with poddin' those peas next," she added over her shoulder, when it seemed like Bridget might be slowing down in the hope of a breather.

With a sigh, Mrs Grimes reiterated the little she recalled about Kate's mother, Laura, on the few occasions she had come to call at the house in Leeds. "Henry, yer brother, were just a babby," she recalled, "the first time yer Mam came here."

She went on to tell Kate about her mother – her stature so similar to her sister's, her hair, her voice, but – she always finished up by telling Kate, "Her eyes were summ'at else. So clear an' grey, like lookin' int' pool a' watter. Just like yours..." and at this she smiled down at Kate and put her arm about her shoulders, giving her a squeeze of comfort. They talked for a few more minutes before a bell tinkled urgently and Mrs Grimes gave a sigh, hauling herself out of her chair and barked at Bridget, "Get tea tray an' take't through. Off ye go! And take some o' that gingerbread."

Bridget became all of a fluster and simultaneously clattered about with the teacups while adding teaspoons to the tray, in preparation for carrying it through to the ladies in the drawing room. After all was in place, she turned to add the final items – two starched and immaculately pressed linen napkins. Her eyes met with Kate's and suddenly the blood seemed to drain from Bridget's face. Without Mrs Grimes seeing her, she hastily crossed herself, then grabbed the tea tray with trembling hands and carried it out of the kitchen. It was not the first time Kate had seen her do that, but she never knew why Bridget seemed to be so agitated in her presence.

"What do you know about Bridget?" asked Kate.

"How d'ye mean? Well, she's been 'ere nigh on five years, came as slip of a girl o' fifteen. Don't really know why we kept 'er on, 'er being such a scatterbrain, but she's a willin' lass, e'en though. T'would be a cruel thing to give 'er notice and she's no bother. Does as she's tell't – eventually," she added with a chuckle. "Ah think she's from t' south of that there Ireland. Took me ages t' understand the girl – but we rub along well enough now. An' I think Harry, the baker's lad is sweet on 'er," Mrs Grimes added with a conspiratorial wink. "Ah spotted 'em in t' park on one of 'er Sunday afternoons off."

"But wouldn't Aunt Eliza be angry if she were courting?" asked Kate, her eyes widening.

"That she would. T'is not proper for a girl of her station to be carryin' on wi' a lad! Ee – but, we were all of us young once…" she added, wistfully.

Kate got the impression that Mrs Grimes had some sympathy for Bridget and dared to ask about how she had met Mr Grimes and what had happened to him.

"Now, now – that's not a story for 'ee. Suffice t' say, he gone now, and me a widder woman so ah'm thankful to 'ave this position. Ah've been wi' the Atkinsons since they married and moved to their first 'ome. An' ah hope to be 'ere for many long years t'come!"

They were interrupted by the kitchen door swinging open as Bridget returned and looking down at her feet, scuttled past Kate and resumed her duties at the kitchen table.

"Reet lass, off 'ee go. We've a meal to get ready for t'night. Miss Rebecca's gentleman and his father will be joining the master and mistress for dinner. Master Frederick won't be back till late, so we'll leave 'im a cold collation on a tray. What about 'ee? Will ah get Bridget to bring your dinner up t' yer room?"

"May I have it down here?" asked Kate, thinking of sitting alone in the gloomy nursery at the top of the house.

"Well, just don't let them 'ear about it. Ah'm sure they'd not be pleased to 'ear 'ow much time ye spend down 'ere," Mrs Grimes warned.

"I really don't think they'd mind," Kate replied, but added silently to herself. "I think this is where they think I belong...."

Stuffing her hands into the pockets of her pinafore, Kate left the kitchen and slipped through the hall and up the stairs, making as little sound as possible in case Aunt Eliza heard her. But the refined tinkle of the ladies' laughter wafted up from the drawing room and Kate let out the breath she had been holding. Laying her hand on the polished banister, she crept up to the next landing and onward, up the narrower stair that led to the top floor. Her fingers curled around the shell she always carried in her pocket, and she sat on the edge of her bed as a silent tear slipped slowly down her cheek.

*****

Kate brushed the tear away with the back of her hand and looked down at the floor. The bright zigzag patterns of the kilim rug startled her and she snapped up her head to stare about her at the discarded toys and dusty books. Instead the pastel wallpaper, the bedhead with LED lights strung across it and the buzzing of her phone jarred her senses. Her head began to spin and she had to fight back the feeling of nausea it created. Taking a few deep breaths, she forced the feeling away and turned to focus on her phone, still buzzing on her bedside table. It was Gran. Stretching out to reach it, she realised that she still held the cockle shell in her hand. Unaware of why it was there, she dropped it on the bedcover and grasped the phone.

"Hi Kate! Just to let you know I've finished up here and thought you might fancy a late lunch if you haven't eaten? And it's brightening up here too so we could go to the bistro down by the river and eat outside if you fancy it?"

"Er… thanks Gran. Yes – that sounds great… Just let me get changed and I'll be there in about half an hour," Kate muttered.

"You OK? You sound a bit – well, funny. What have you been doing?"

"Oh I'm fine. Just been dozing and I'm not fully *compos*," Kate hastily replied. "I'll see you there. You get us a table and I'll be there soon."

"OK! Bye," and the phone clicked off, leaving Kate bewildered and still shaking.

CHAPTER TWELVE

1891 Hull

Amid all the hubbub and excitement, Aunt Eliza had retired to the new drawing room and Kate knelt by her administering some smelling salts from a small silver container.

"How do you feel now Aunt?" asked Kate, as she rubbed the back of her aunt's hand.

"Better, thank you Kate. This is all too much. See if you can find Mrs Grimes and ask her if she might be able to send through some tea," her aunt replied in a shaky voice.

Kate stood and closed the drawing room door quietly behind her, trying rather unsuccessfully to drown out the noise of clattering and banging, shouts and muttered curses as the removal men heaved trunks and bulky furniture items up the steps and into their new home. A brass plaque fixed to each of the pillars outside the front door proclaimed 'Dalton House'. Mrs Grimes had already thrown it a glance and sniffed as she made a mental note to send out Ellen, one of the new housemaids, to give the brass a good going-over.

Charles Atkinson's business empire was going from strength to strength, and as many of his new interests were based around the ports of Goole and Hull, he felt he needed to be closer to where his commercial interests lay. He was now Director of two companies and on the Board of three more, as well as having a hand in a few other subsidiary ones all dealing in the import, export and transportation of raw materials and associated building products, which were either made locally and needed transporting to feed the ever-growing industries of the North, or else were arriving almost daily from Britain and overseas.

And with that came an elevated status which required a more ostentatious house and so had necessitated the move to Hull which, he assured Eliza, was absolutely necessary and in line with their position in society.

Aunt Eliza had been less impressed but of course, she had to go along with her husband's wishes and soon they were the new owners of Dalton House, a Georgian-façaded house in an area of similar buildings in a quiet curving street far away from the grimy noisy dock area and with a small, enclosed area of gardens opposite for the use of the residents. Frederick was now learning to be an engineer in a business owned by a business colleague of Uncle Charles. In time Charles had aspirations that his son's skills would be an asset to the commercial opportunities that were opening up in the area. It seemed a very long time ago that Charles had once been glad to shake the hand of Kate's father, William Hoxton, the barge owner and draw up a contract to transport goods to York, Selby, Leeds and Goole by the rivers and canals.

Kate could barely remember those days but if she thought back, the image that always came to mind was the fateful night on the river eight years ago when they were bringing her father's body in the simple coffin back to York. Imprinted on her mind was the look of anguish on her mother's face as she held her children close. Henry had been trying not to cry and Kate, then aged six, was holding tightly onto her rag doll. The night had been bitterly cold and rain and sleet had blown horizontally into their faces as they boarded the barge. Their mother had ushered them quickly into the cramped little cabin at the back of the boat and shut the door tightly to keep in what little heat there was.

Somewhere at the back of Kate's memory there was another presence, another voice that seemed to have no source, but yet surrounded her. She couldn't understand why the others did not hear it but she did not dare question her mother who she recalled, was sitting hunched on one of the benches with her head bowed and one arm around Henry. Kate wanted to see who was calling, who was expecting her to answer, who was offering words of comfort and yet demanding a response. But instead, she responded to her mother's gesture and stepped forward to be enfolded into her mother's embrace.

Kate was abruptly brought back to the present as the crash of broken china rang out from the kitchen. It was followed by raised voices and Kate recognised that of Mrs Grimes in full flow and the retort from one of the youths transporting the crates and boxes below stairs. Kate was reluctant to interrupt and ask Mrs Grimes for tea to be brought to Aunt Eliza but nevertheless, braved the storm below and ran down the few stairs and pushed open the swing door into the kitchen. The sight that met her was enough to make anyone gasp. A full box of the best bone china had ended up on the slate-tiled floor. The light glinted off the golden edging on the broken pieces of delicately patterned porcelain, pinks and greens delicately painted but now lying in a heap of odd-shaped fragments amongst the straw that had been packed around it in the hope of saving it from such a fate. Mrs Grimes' face was puce, the youth's face was grey and the two housemaids were standing looking like matching statues, their mouths open wide in perfect 'O's and their hands clapped to their cheeks.

Kate couldn't help herself and reached forward and bent down to try to retrieve some whole pieces from the catastrophic heap in front of her. Seeing her do so, Mary and Ellen, the two housemaids, joined her and between them managed to assemble a mismatched selection of cups, plates and saucers. By now Mrs Grimes was shooing the youth out of her kitchen via the back door which led onto the side of the house.

"Aunt Eliza would like some tea sent up to the drawing room, Mrs Grimes," Kate began hesitantly. Seeing her look in response she added, "But I'm sure between us Mary and I can get a tray together while you supervise the rest of the removals." Mrs

Grimes was about to remonstrate with her but then looked at her with wordless thanks. Thrusting a brush into Ellen's hand, Mrs Grimes set to making good the scene of chaos in front of them while Mary searched out the kettle and set it on one of the new gas-fired stoves. Thankfully it was soon boiling and leaving Mary to complete the task, Kate returned to her aunt in the drawing room, dodging the men struggling with large items of furniture and overstuffed boxes entering the front door. Another pair were in the process of getting one of the bedroom wardrobes up the staircase, which they did with much grunting and muttered oaths.

*****

Over the next few weeks the family settled into Dalton House. Aunt Eliza and Uncle Charles had the large bedroom on the first floor facing the front of the house. It sported a large bay window which overlooked the park and had a dressing room attached which delighted Aunt Eliza. Uncle Charles had converted one of the bedrooms on that floor to become a bathroom which had a large bath with an inbuilt shower attached. Aunt Eliza was unsure of using such a contraption but Uncle Charles assured her it was the height of fashion and beneficial to both the health and constitution of the user, especially if a cold shower concluded the soak in a hot bath. Aunt Eliza remained unconvinced. On that floor was a smaller bedroom that Uncle Charles used if he was coming home late and did not want to disturb her.

Frederick also had rooms on the first floor but to the side of the house and to his bedroom was attached a smaller room he used as a study cum office where he could shut himself away, poring over his engineering manuals and technical drawings. In addition there was a bedroom kept for guests.

The ground floor of the house held the library, Uncle Charles' study, the drawing room and a large imposing dining room, while the kitchen, pantry and larder were all below stairs and towards the back of the house so that tradesmen could make their deliveries unseen from the street.

Kate was assigned a modest-sized bedroom on the second floor with a small window that also looked out over the small park opposite and the street between. It was comfortable and had all that Kate needed – a dresser and wash-stand, a wardrobe, a chair and small desk and a trunk in which was stored any items not required for the time of year. Gone were the dusty toys and leftover childhood items. Instead she had a small bookcase and a shelf on which she put a few knick-knacks she had collected over the years. Next to her room was a small lavatory and further along the corridor, beyond the stairs, were several large presses which held linens and spare bedding. At the far end was the room Mrs Grimes occupied. Finally, there were two attic rooms above for the two housemaids.

It was a comfortable home for a well-to-do family of means and aspirations – exactly what Uncle Charles wished to convey to the great and the good of the growing city of Hull. The port had grown and expanded over the years, assuring it the reputation of being able to handle goods from the Britain and abroad. The River Ouse finished its land journey at Goole and fed into the Humber estuary, which was both tidal and shallow causing it to be muddy and thus requiring frequent dredging. The docks had been dug deep to accommodate ships both large and small from all around the world which might come there to offload their exotic cargoes of hard woods from Africa or the Far East, silks and satins from the Low Countries, fruit from the Caribbean or raw materials from the manufacturing countries across the North Sea. It sent coal and iron made in the nearby industrial cities, woollen cloth woven in the mills of Yorkshire and Lancashire, china goods from the Potteries and cutlery from the factories in and around Sheffield. The docks were never still, always bustling with noise and the sound of machinery and men at work. And it was as he stood and surveyed this eruption of activity that Uncle Charles felt a sense of pride for what he had achieved in his life, coming from humble beginnings and using his innate business acumen to build a little empire for his family and the generations yet to come. A self-made man – the phrase sat well on him.

Kate had few clear memories of Hull. She knew that, with her mother and brother, she had come here to bring back her father's body when he died. She remembered that frantic train journey from York when her mother received the news that her husband was ill. He had succumbed to a sickness in his chest, exacerbated by the damp cold of a trip down river in December. She and Henry had not been allowed to see their father when he died so she had only the vaguest feeling of loss. The journey back to York by barge – well, that was a different matter – and one she pushed to the back of her mind whenever it threatened to surface, usually in the quiet moments in the dark of night.

Her schooling was over now. She was fifteen years old and not particularly academic. She could read, write and do arithmetic adequately but she never entertained any thoughts of more advanced skills. After all her lot would be, no doubt, to manage a home of her own one day. The one thing she could do more than adequately was sew. She had spent enough time with Aunt Eliza as they stitched and embroidered by the fireside. She could turn a neat seam, slip an almost invisible hem, pleat and smock, gather and ruffle so neatly that she had hand made presents for her aunt and cousin Becky for their Christmases – not least of all because she had no income of her own with which to buy items. But it gave her pleasure and her work was always admired by the recipients, especially when they discovered the neatly stitched initials worked into the corners of the items, be they handkerchiefs or nightdress cases.

One late spring morning, a few weeks after their arrival in Hull, Kate donned her bonnet and cape and stepped out into the sunshine as it flickered through the fresh green leaves of the trees in the small park opposite. Her aunt had asked if she could return a book that a friend had lent her, as she was up to her eyes trying to plan a dinner party that Uncle Charles had decided they needed to have to entertain some of his new associates and their wives. Kate had left her and Mrs Grimes worrying over menus and deciding what was in season and what was appropriate to impress their guests.

'Poor Aunt Eliza', Kate thought to herself. She was in such a state, what with making sure the house and furnishings looked the part and then deciding on what to serve their guests, quite sure that it would be remarked upon in company after the event. As for what she should wear…!

Having returned the book to Aunt Eliza's friend who lived in the adjoining street, Kate hopped on to one of the horse-drawn trams that ran along Holderness Road and having paid her one penny fare, she made her way on to the top deck and surveyed the view. It was a fine day and luckily the wind was from the north-west so that the more noxious smells from the docks and manufacturing areas of the town were not in evidence. Leaving behind the open spaces to the east of the town, the tram headed into the built-up areas of crowded housing. From her vantage point she noted the rows and rows of terraced houses and occasionally an alley running between them allowed a view of yet another identical row. These were the homes of the many workers who laboured on the railways or in the various docks of the port.

Alighting at Witham, she decided to head across the North Bridge and into the shopping area of the town. She had no conscious memory of the place, yet she felt a strange familiarity and awareness of having a connection to it. Her feet seemed to lead her on, and without thinking she turned down toward the river which made its sluggish progress beneath her.

She could hear the sound of a train leaving the dock area, loaded with timber, recently unloaded from the ships lying in the Victoria Dock. But there were other sounds, all jostling for her attention. Shouts, crashes, discordant screeches of machinery, rumbling, a shrill whistle, the rhythmic clatter of the railway trucks passing close by. And another more subtle, more distant sound – hardly distinguishable unless the ear was tuned to its sibilant whispering tone.

At last…
You've come – at last.
It has been a long time.
But not for me…
Time is nothing to me. I have been here for ever.
But enough about me.
Have you come to renew an old friendship?

Kate turned her head to try to locate the source but could not. There was no one close enough. A cold shiver ran down her spine despite the spring warmth of the sun. Some deep-seated recollection pushed up from the depths of her memory and crawled up her spine, wrapping itself around her mind.

Where are you?

Who are you?

Don't you know?
Don't you remember?

Leave me alone…

Go away. I don't know you!

Ah – but you do.
And I know you.
It's like we are … family…

Kate took to her heels and ran back over the bridge, diving

into the throng of people heading across the road and dodging between the press of horse-drawn carts and hand-held barrows heading in all directions at the road junction. She did not stop until she had put a few streets between her and – what? She couldn't comprehend what had just occurred but all she knew was that she wanted to put as much distance as possible between '*it*' and her.

CHAPTER THIRTEEN

1891 Hull

The Atkinson's first dinner party had gone off quite well but very quickly, Aunt Eliza realised that she needed to raise her sights as regards the latest fashions and décor. Uncle Charles seemed oblivious as he poured out the port and passed round the cigars after dinner to the gentlemen who had remained at the dining table after the ladies had withdrawn. There was much guffawing and raucous conversation from what Kate could hear, leaning on the banisters on the landing above the hall. Naturally Kate was not part of the company, although Frederick was well-ensconced with the men as Uncle Charles' sole intention was to introduce him to some of the local businessmen who might look favourably upon him in the future.

Kate let out a sigh and climbed the stairs to her room, the sound of the men's laughter and the ladies tinkling polite amusement growing fainter with every step. Mrs Grimes had made her up a tray, which Ellen had brought up to her room after the ladies had retired to the drawing room. Kate might have felt bitter. She might have thought to herself, 'Fit only for scraps and leftovers', but she knew that she would never be included in that way. Sitting by her little desk at the window, now shrouded in the heavy drapes that shut out the night, she realised that she would have to make her own way in life. Her aunt and uncle had been very kind to her and taken her in when no-one else had, but she would not be following in her cousin Becky's footsteps, making an advantageous marriage under their guidance and management. She needed to review her future. She could not live here forever, destined to become an old spinster sitting in the corner. She needed to consider what her options were.

Her schooling had been adequate – she could read and write, manage figures and do simple arithmetic – enough to manage the running of a household. A housekeeper's position might be appropriate but she was far too young; people wanted an older and more mature woman – like Mrs Grimes, she smiled to herself. She could start at the bottom and work as a housemaid but she felt that was beneath her – and what would Aunt Eliza think of that! With a sigh, she realised there were so very few options open to her. The one thing she could do well was sewing and with a flash of insight, she realised that perhaps that that was the skill she must hone for the future. But now, some cold roast beef and sliced ham called and she would concentrate on that for the moment.

*****

The following morning the family slept late and it was nearly eleven before the bell calling for breakfast was heard in the kitchen. Everyone had had a long night. Both of the maids and Mrs Grimes had been up into the early hours washing pots and pans and clearing the dining room. Ellen had already been up for a few hours as her daily task was making up the fires, so it was a weary young housemaid who flopped into one of the wooden chairs in the kitchen for a moment's respite before Mrs Grimes instructed her on next list of tasks for the day. Mary, the other housemaid, had been sent off to the market to get some fresh produce in preparation for another day of producing meals for the household. Everyone looked weary and the gloomy day and grey drizzle that fell only seemed to dull everyone's spirits. The gaslights had already had to be lit in the kitchen and in the hallway and as the family started coming downstairs, Ellen was shooed out of her chair and sent to illuminate the dining room in preparation for breakfast.

As it turned out, only Charles and Frederick made an appearance and thick heads were obviously the order of the day. Uncle Charles frowned as the clatter of plates and cutlery heralded the serving of kippers and scrambled eggs, but Frederick seemed unfazed and tucked into his plateful. Kate had already eaten in the kitchen as none of the family had appeared at the usual time. She was about to head into the drawing room to collect her embroidery when she heard the tinkle of the bell signalling Aunt Eliza's requirement for breakfast to be brought to her room.

"I'll take it up," Kate said, as she popped her head round the kitchen door.

"Thank 'ee pet," said Mrs Grimes gratefully, rising to answer the back door to direct the coal deliveryman to the shed outside.

After knocking gently on Aunt Eliza's door, Kate slowly pushed it open and quietly laid the tray on the bedside table. Aunt Eliza wasn't taken aback as Kate often brought her tray up to her. Padding over the Turkish rug that lay upon the wooden floor, Kate slid back the heavy curtains and noted that the room did not brighten much due to the overcast day outside.

"Shall I light the lamp?" asked Kate.

"Please," replied Aunt Eliza, "But not too bright."

Handing her aunt her pelisse, Kate rearranged the covers and waited till there was space ready to set down the tray. Aunt Eliza did not eat a large breakfast so the tray held a teacup, teapot, small milk jug and sugar bowl and a silver toast rack with four small triangles of toast. A glass pot of home-made preserve completed the repast.

"How did the dinner party go last night? Did you make the acquaintance of some interesting ladies?" asked Kate.

"Well, my dear, I don't know about interesting, but I can see I shall have to familiarise myself very soon with what is going on in Hull society. And, I am ashamed to say, I fear I did not meet up with their approval as regards my attire. One lady took pity on me, I think, and kindly gave me the name of her dressmaker and suggested I pay her a visit. She considers her the very best in the town and seemingly she has illustrations of all the latest French fashions from which to order an outfit. Charles may not see such expense well-spent but if he wishes to make an impression in this town, I can see that it is the ladies we will have to impress."

"Where is this dressmaker?" Kate asked, surprised as she thought her aunt had looked divine last night in a an off-the-shoulder dark green silk outfit with lace trims and ruffled sleeves.

"It is on the card over there on my dressing table," Aunt Eliza pointed across the room.

"Numbers 1 and 2 Kingston Square – Madame Clapham" Kate read from the small white embossed card.

"I think I shall have to pay her a call very soon…" sighed Aunt Eliza.

*****

"May I come with you, Aunt?" ventured Kate the next morning as her aunt prepared to head into town to visit Madame Clapham's establishment.

Eliza considered for a moment and then agreed. "We may as well find our way around this town together. And you may help me carry anything we might purchase. Go and get your coat and hat and I shall ask Mary to hail a cab for us both."

Having given the cab driver the appropriate address, they set off into town. The more open housing gave way to tightly packed and meaner dwellings as they approached the dock area and then crossed over one of the bridges into the central part of town. Turning off Jarratt Street they entered a quiet square and the cab stopped at the first building on the corner where a sign proclaimed 'Claphams'. Having paid their fare, Aunt Eliza led the way up a flight of stone steps to an imposing doorway. At their approach the door was held open by a bell boy of about fourteen, Kate guessed, dressed in a smart suit. Upon his head was a small round brimless hat under which twinkled a pair of mischievous eyes, a button nose and a cheeky grin. After they had entered, he resumed his post just outside the door and awaited the next customer.

As they went in, they were greeted by a distinguished-looking woman with piercing blue eyes and blonde hair, piled up upon her head. She wore an elegant tight-fitting black silk two-piece suit with just a ruffle of a white collar showing at her neck. The puffed leg-o'-mutton sleeves were tapered to her wrists and her only jewellery was a long set of black beads from which hung a small pair of lorgnettes. They were ushered into the foyer where Aunt Eliza was offered a seat. Having introduced herself as the eponymous 'Madame Clapham' and ascertained the reason for their visit, Madame enquired whether there was a requirement for outfits for both *'Moddum'* and 'the young lady'? Aunt Eliza assured her that it was only herself in need of some fashionable ensembles. With an almost imperceptible sniff in Kate's direction, Madame C. led Aunt Eliza upstairs to where Kate could only imagine there would be models and fitting rooms for the clients. As she reached the head of the stairs, Aunt Eliza turned and said, "Just wait there for me, my dear," and then disappeared from view.

Kate sat on a chair in a corner where she could see the comings and goings, but still be fairly unobtrusive. Occasionally a seamstress would appear from another door and go upstairs carrying some gorgeous fabric, a tape measure draped around her neck. After a while she would reappear and scuttle down the stairs clutching a sheaf of papers and head back through the same door into, what Kate could only assume, was the workroom area.

Kate had plenty of time to look around. The walls had tastefully framed drawings of elegant gowns, stating that they were exclusive to this establishment and designed to echo the most up to date modes from the fashion houses of London and Paris. Elegant day dresses, richly embroidered and bejewelled ballgowns, smart walking suits featuring ankle-length skirts with matching jackets. Parasols and fabulous hats completed the outfits. Kate was utterly captivated by the sheer variety of styles on show.

After what seemed an eternity Aunt Eliza reappeared, followed by Madame C.

"I will be in touch shortly to arrange a final fitting for the outfits and we should be able to have these delivered by the end of next week if that is convenient," Madame announced as they both descended the stairs.

"Perfectly," replied Aunt Eliza.

"Would *moddum* like to set up an account?"

Aunt Eliza gushed, "Absolutely, yes. I shall ask Mr Atkinson to contact you later today and do so. I am much obliged to you, Madame and thank you for your excellent service. Good day."

"Good day, *moddum*. Thank you for your esteemed custom. William – show the lady out please!" barked Madame to the bell boy standing by the doorway.

At that, Aunt Eliza beckoned to Kate and led the way out and down the steps into the street. The bell boy dared to give Kate a wink, but she turned her head disdainfully and followed her aunt.

CHAPTER FOURTEEN

1892 Hull

The months passed and soon winter was upon them. Kate's sixteenth birthday was in early February and the family had arranged for a little celebration. As Kate had no real friends to invite, it was a simple family affair. Becky and her husband were now proud parents to two young children and lived in Leeds, so had indicated that they would not be able to travel, especially with the weather, the children, the pressure of work, and so on.

Frederick was nearly twenty-two and already making his way in the world, far too self-absorbed to be bothered with his young cousin's birthday but, nevertheless, he had left a beribboned parcel on the breakfast table at her place for her to open that morning. Inside was a silver locket with an engraved design of filigree scrolls and swirls.

Mrs Grimes baked a wonderful cake and so it was that it was only Kate's aunt and uncle who sat down to tea with her that afternoon and wished her 'Happy Birthday'. After tea, Uncle Charles produced a large parcel wrapped in brown paper and string. He had added a red satin bow (courtesy of his wife's sewing basket) in an attempt to make it look more cheerful. Kate carefully undid the string and folded back the paper, smoothing it as she went.

Inside was a wooden box, the polished surface reflecting the gaslights flickering around the room, already lit on such a grey February day. As she laid it in front of her, she could see that there was a little key with a green silk tassel protruding from the brass escutcheon at the front of the box. Smiling excitedly at

Uncle Charles, she turned the key and opened up the lid. As she did so, it lay back upon the table and became a writing slope.

"Oh, Uncle Charles – it's beautiful! Thank you so much!" Kate exclaimed, running her hands over the pristine leather coverings of both halves of the slope. Her fingers explored the little compartments and she was even more delighted to find a beautiful silver pen holder in one, a silver stamp box in the other and, under one of the leather flaps, a sheaf of thick creamy writing paper. When she closed the box again, she was delighted to find a matching brass plate set into the lid, left blank so that one day she could have her initials added, if she so wished.

Later that evening, as Kate sat on her bed and brushed her hair, she looked across at the box sitting on her table by the window. She went over and stroked the smooth mahogany edges and ran her fingertips over the brass plate, dreaming of the initials she might one day be able to add to it. 'Perhaps her married name?' she mused. Another thought came to her and she opened the desk drawer and moving aside some odds and ends, found a screwed-up piece of tissue paper. Reverently she unwrapped it and sat the cockle shell on the palm of her hand. Thoughts of her mother and brother flooded back to her, and misty fragments of memories of her part in their demise. She sat for a while, lost in contemplation before she shivered involuntarily and opened the box. Her searching fingers explored the inbuilt compartments which held the pen and stamp box. Sliding them over to the other side she tried to lift the leather flap using the little cloth loop set into the leather. Another cavity opened up, but it was the edges that her fingers explored. 'Did it? Might it?' She hardly dared to hope. But then, at the pressure of her finger, the wooden edge gave slightly and she pressed down further. A little lever was hidden underneath and by sliding her nail under the edge she could push it over, exposing a secret compartment beneath. Her discovery filled her with delight. And then she knew exactly what would fit in there – as if it was just made for it…

*****

Why Kate packed the writing slope box into the already stuffed back seat of Gran's car was a mystery to her. But somehow, she wanted to have it with her. No doubt Jen would scoff but so what? 'Maybe I could write up notes on it,' she mused. Then she caught herself on – 'What's a laptop for you idiot! This is the twenty-first century!' Again that unwelcome shiver ran down her spine before she shook it off, grabbed her fleece and sweatshirt and jammed them around the box to keep it safe in transit.

The best part of another year in York was ahead of her and there was the usual mix of anticipation, trepidation, exhilaration, and probable exhaustion ahead. The sound of Gran's voice caused her to look up and she gave her a thumbs-up. Everything was packed, she could close the cottage door – they were ready to go.

CHAPTER FIFTEEN

1892 Hull

As I grew older, I began to realise that I didn't really know where I fitted. I could not go on living with them indefinitely and yet, how was I to make my own way in life? An advantageous marriage was not on the cards for me, having no claim on my Uncle's growing fortune. I would bring no prestige, power or position to such an arrangement. I was merely the poor relation, in every sense of the word. I sat down with Uncle Charles on one of the few evenings when he was able to stretch out in front of the fire and relax, rather than shutting himself away in his study or attending meetings and coming home late, reeking of stale cigar smoke and slightly inebriated. I broached the subject of what, if anything, my parents had been able to leave me in the way of means. Uncle Charles took a deep breath, and looked down at his hands, considering his answer.

"My dear Kate, I fear you came to us with nothing bar the clothes you stood up in and the few items your step-aunt and uncle passed over to me the day I came to collect you at your Aunt Eliza's bidding. She insisted that her youngest sister's child should not be left to be brought up in, as she put it, some hovel in the backstreets of York."

I remember feeling rather confused until I recalled that it was my mother's previous brother-in-law and his wife who had originally claimed me after the … accident. They were the Shiptons, my mother having been widowed when her husband George Shipton, my half-brother Henry's father, was drowned. I remembered very little of them, but I did recall that the woman was very brusque and had an unusually beaky nose. Why that should have remained in my memory, I had no idea.

Uncle Charles continued, "When your father, William Hoxton, died, your mother Laura was left with many debts and debtors. She was a good businesswoman, your mother, and I have no doubt that she would have been able to set all your father's affairs in order but ..." and here his voice trailed off.

"I understand, Uncle," I responded. "She was taken and so was Henry, so the affairs would have been so very much more complicated, I imagine."

"Indeed," he nodded, slowly, making a church steeple of his fingers as he bent his head and let silence fill the void for the next few minutes.

Clearing his throat, he lifted his head and quietly added, "After the lawyer in York had sorted through all the paperwork and accounts, and that took the best part of a year to do, what with all the people who had accounts to pay and those who needed paying, the boats had to be sold to pay off the outstanding loans on them. The home you lived in was rented and the few pieces of furniture and household items were auctioned off, to help with the outstanding debts accrued. I went up to York that day and it was a sad affair to watch. I won't tell you anymore, I've no wish to upset you ... Suffice to say, that at the end of it all, a few pounds were sent over by Mr Marr the solicitor, and these, we put in an account at the bank for you until you were of an age when you needed them."

"I should have liked to have been able to bring something from my home ..." my voice trailed off. But then, I had only been six or seven and I'm not even sure what I might have salvaged. I shook my head to clear the unhappy thoughts. "Uncle, you and Aunt Eliza have been very kind to let me live with you. But I shall have to think about my future."

"Now, now, my dear. No more talk of that – not yet," and with that Uncle stood and held out his arms so that I might bury my head in his chest, the rough woollen tweed of his jacket bristling against my cheek. How could I feel so alone with such a dear man as this?

*****

The cold wind snatched at the wisps of hair that had escaped my bonnet and I clamped my hand upon it to keep it from being snatched from my head, even though I had tied the ribbons firmly. I looked about me, unsure of where my steps had taken me and having no recall of my journey to this spot. The road ran downhill, away from me, and in the distance I could see through the gap in the buildings where the river emptied endlessly in a muddy flow into the docks. It was the sound of running boots that first roused me, metal-studded soles clattering on the cobbles, and arms pushing me aside, out of the way. Almost exclusively men's voices, raised in alarm and at their clamour, heads turned and others swelled their ranks, jostling each other in their haste to reach their goal.

What the motivation was for their haste, I could not comprehend, but it had caused faces to contort in alarm and tasks to be abandoned. I was torn between joining the growing throng heading down the hill or escaping this noise and frenzy. In the end, rough hands pushing me aside and a gruff shout made up my mind. This was no place to be, amongst a rabble, a mob. Their emotion and rising panic transferred itself to me, and my breathing became faster as their anxiety transferred itself to me.

I turned and pressed myself against the nearest wall, the solid red bricks giving me support until my shaking legs felt able to take me away from this scene. Turning a corner, I escaped the rush of humanity heading toward me, and the sight of the empty lane was momentarily comforting. But then I had to find a way out of this maelstrom and reach a place of familiarity.

With still no sense of which way to turn, I headed uphill and away from the dock area, hoping that I would soon find myself in a familiar street or in sight of a familiar landmark. A church came into view at a crossroads of two broader streets and I recognised I was approaching Hessle Road. The clattering of a tram galvanised me into action and with relief I was able to board it and head away from this nightmare.

Indeed, I wondered at first if this was a nightmare, a terrifying dream, but the immediacy of the sounds around me, the hard seat upon which I perched and the rattle and sway of the tram made me quickly doubt that. This was reality. But I had no recollection of getting here, wherever 'here' was, nor what had occurred. With relief I saw the familiar buildings of the town centre approaching and my breathing began to relax. A latent feeling of nausea persisted and my heavy clothes seemed far too constricting. I tugged at my high neckline and pulled my shawl away from my throat in an attempt to allow some cooler air to soothe my damp and burning skin.

*****

Aunt Eliza was unaware of what had happened until Frederick came home later that evening looking exhausted, dishevelled and gaunt. As I stood on the landing at the top of the stairs, I could see him enter the front door. He took a moment to draw a deep breath, as if to steady himself, but was unaware of me out of sight above him. He threw his hat down on the hall stand and walked over to the drawing room door, pausing momentarily before he thought better of entering and went instead into Uncle Charles' study. A few moments later he reappeared, wiping his mouth with the back of his hand. In his other hand he held a small glass of what I thought looked like brandy.

Again he paused at the drawing room door, then gently turned the knob and entered, closing the door quietly behind him. From my position at the head of the stairs, unsure whether to follow him into the drawing room, I heard only the murmur of voices, then a pause and finally a loud howl. Galvanised into action, I flew down the carpeted steps, across the tiled hallway and found myself at the door. Pausing for a few moments I could hear the sound of a woman crying and the soothing tones of a male voice. I didn't wait to consider if I would be intruding, but hurriedly opened the door and entered.

Frederick was kneeling beside his mother, his hands wrapped around hers which she gripped together fiercely in her lap. Her body was bent over and she was rocking in time to her anguished sobs.

I flashed a glance at Frederick as he looked up upon my entry and tried to puzzle out what had happened.

"It's Father…" Frederick began, but at the sound of his words, Aunt Eliza renewed her wails and he put his arms around her and held her close.

"Ask Mrs Grimes to fetch the doctor. Mama will need a sedative," his voice staccato and broken.

I threw a quizzical glance at him, but he merely shook his head and I realised I would have to wait for any further explanation.

Frederick sat with his mother until the doctor came and escorted her, with the help of Mrs Grimes, up to her bedroom. Only then did he collapse onto the couch and turn to me.

"It's Father. There has been a terrible accident at the docks. He is missing. We don't know any more."

Then he buried his face in his hands and his shoulders heaved in silent sobs. "And it's all my fault…" he continued.

"But it can't be, Frederick. What's happened?" I sobbed, as I rushed to his side.

But all he would keep repeating was, "It was all my fault…"

CHAPTER SIXTEEN

1892 Hull

Finally I managed to piece together the information that was available and match it to what Frederick was telling us. The morning of the accident, Uncle Charles had set off early down to the St Andrew's Dock where his company was working on the engineering part of adding a new gate. He was proud that Frederick had drawn up the plans, and that this was the first piece of work he would have seen through from the planning stage to its scheduled completion in a few weeks' time. Uncle Charles' company had invested a huge amount of money in the undertaking and were well on target to having it successfully completed on time. The North-Eastern Railway Company were already excavating the land for extending the railway lines to carry goods from the new dock area. They were depending on the undertaking being finished to coincide with their own work.

And so Uncle Charles had set off that morning, not going to his office in town, as was his usual routine, but heading down to the docks to see how the work was progressing. The proud father, stepping out into the morning, head held high, cane swinging in his hand and his immaculately shined boots striding smartly down the cobbled street.

When he arrived, he stood out of sight, surreptitiously watching as Frederick gave orders and took charge of the group of men working on the excavations while the huge pile drivers thundered as they dug deeper into the mud and rock of the dock basin. He managed to get close enough to see Frederick holding a large plan, which he had unfolded and laid out while indicating with a sweep of his hand some indication of the next task and then pointing across the dock to emphasise his directive. A trio of men in work clothes, flat caps upon their heads, withdrew from the group around Frederick and set off about their work. A warm glow spread through Charles' core as he felt pride in what his son had achieved. Going behind some machinery, he inched closer to the dock and marvelled at the progress already made, hugging the warmth of his pride closer and allowing himself a smug smile of paternal satisfaction.

He hardly heard the creak that presaged the destruction of the existing dock gates nor the ensuing rush of water that flooded the dock and drove all before it. It was only as the keel of a boat rose up in front of him that he suddenly became aware of the impending peril and, in the last few seconds, threw up his arms in a vain attempt to protect himself from the ensuing disaster.

Boats, masts, flotsam, bodies, screams, creaks, splintering wood, gushing water, utter devastation. All in a few moments of mayhem. And Charles was gone…

As the water retreated from its surge and all the floating mass of people, boats and wreckage returned to cover the surface of the dock, voices called for help and people responded by throwing ropes and grasping at whatever they could reach, in an attempt to give aid to the drowning fishermen and their families, thrown so brutally into the water.

Only in the hours that followed did it become clear what had happened. And then the accusations and blame were bandied about. The excavations had been too close to the existing gates. The vibrations had loosened the mud and weakened the foundations. The pile drivers were too powerful. The engineers had it all wrong.

*****

Frederick was ashen-faced and covered in mud from helping with the rescue of those thrown into the water or trapped in the wreckage. It was many hours later, as he made to finally leave the scene of carnage, that he was approached by one of the directors who told him that he had seen Charles earlier, heading down to the dock. Had Frederick spoken to him? Where was he now? A cold finger ran down Frederick's spine and panic rose in his stomach. He spent another frantic hour scouring the dock sides and pulling aside heaped-up wreckage but found nothing and no-one. And so he headed home, hoping that the man had been mistaken, that it was not his father that he had seen, that when he arrived home his father would be waiting there with his mother, wondering why Frederick was so late home. But in his heart, he knew. A cold dread filled him as he walked out of the docks and headed towards the hardest task of his life so far.

<u>Strange accident at Hull Dock</u>: An extraordinary accident occurred on Friday morning at Hull Dock. Extensions are being carried on at the St Andrew's Fish Dock, belonging to the North-Eastern Railway Company. These extensions take the form of a new dock, to be connected with the old one by a gate. The new dock had practically been finished, and the caisson fixed to prevent water from getting in, but early on Friday morning, however, the dock gates gave way entirely. It was high water at the time, and so great was the rush that several keels were sunk, and practically every vessel in the dock broke from its moorings, and they were jammed into a hopeless mass of wreckage. The dock presents an extraordinary sight, and the police, together with dock authorities, are instituting inquiries and search to see if any persons have been drowned or injured. A later telegram from Hull states that the accident is more serious than first appeared. Almost all the vessels moored in St Andrew's Dock broke away, and, in addition to the two keels sunk, and a smack that was broken up, many other vessels were seriously damaged. Two or three smacks were so damaged as to be useless for the future. Fortunately, no loss of life was caused, though, at first, it was feared that a considerable number of persons had perished. Both women and children were on the sunken vessels but they were, without difficulty, rescued. Those on board the vessels had a narrow escape

from drowning. The collapse of the gate is owing to hidden springs being freed by pile driving and excavation. The damage is estimated at considerably over £100,000.
23 October 1892 - Hull Daily Mail, Yorkshire

*****

The whole household barely slept that night, Kate more so as she relived the events of earlier in the day. She had told no-one of her experiences that morning, nor of her proximity to the awful event. As she lay in the darkness, willing herself to sleep but fearful of seeing the scenes replay behind her closed eyelids and hearing the sounds echo in the recesses of her mind, she thought she could hear the merest whisper of another, more insistent voice insinuating itself between the shouts and screams.

A quieter, softer, yet more audible one, not overshadowed by the others nor drowned out by their strident tones. It came from a different place yet pushed aside the others in its bid to be heard. She didn't have to strain to make out the words, nor turn her head, the better to locate the source. It came from nowhere, and everywhere, it was within her yet, not.

I am glad you were there.
I didn't know if you would come at my summons.
You have been quite difficult to reach.
But I knew we would soon meet.

Go away.

You know you want to hear me.
An old friend said you would come.
You met him long ago.

Leave me alone...

I thought perhaps that was the best way...
To get your attention.

What did you do?

Oh, just a small display of what I am capable of.
Please come again.
We have much to talk about, little one.

CHAPTER SEVENTEEN

1893 Hull

In the months after Uncle Charles' death, with the family in deep mourning as was the custom, few visitors came to the house and those that did either presented their cards at the door and were politely shown away, or else were admitted as they had to discuss arrangements or business affairs with Aunt Eliza and Frederick.

The will was read a few weeks after the lavish funeral, Uncle Charles' body having eventually been found many days later, deeply buried in the mud and wreckage of the dock. The solicitor came to the house and was shown into the drawing room by Mrs Grimes, followed soon after by Frederick with Aunt Eliza leaning heavily on his arm, swathed in black silk, lace and a net covering her face. Kate was in her room when Ellen knocked on her door and told her that she was to come downstairs to the drawing room. Upon entering she could see her aunt and Frederick together upon the couch, his hands laced tightly together and hanging between his knees, his head bent. Her aunt held a flimsy lace handkerchief to her nose, her eyes red-rimmed and puffy. The sibilant tones of the solicitor's voice summoned Kate to an upright chair opposite the family, his manner austere and sombre. As she did so, she could see various documents laid out upon the side table and others folded and tied with ribbon in the leather satchel at his side.

"Young lady," he began, "you have been asked to attend this family meeting as you have an interest in your late Uncle's will."

"Do I?" Kate asked, somewhat bewildered, unaccustomed to how such matters were dealt with.

"Yes," he continued, "your uncle made some provision for you which is not dependent on the assets of the family or his businesses. He set aside a small amount of money for you in a trust, to be released to you upon your coming of age at twenty-one, or upon his death, should that predate it, provided you were over eighteen. Your cousin Frederick was to provide for you until such a time."

Kate sat, straight backed and wide-eyed as she took in the words he uttered in a monotonous and sombre tone.

He continued, "As I understand, you have not reached the age of eighteen?" and here he paused to look over his pince-nez spectacles, awaiting Kate's small nod of assent, "Therefore, you will be under your cousin Frederick's care."

At that point, Kate was dismissed as the solicitor announced that there were 'no other items pertinent to her remaining'. Kate stood, and with a quick glance at her aunt and cousin, quietly left the room, shutting the door soundlessly behind her.

As she returned to her room, she recalled the conversation she had had with Uncle Charles and how he had informed her that the small amount of money remaining after her family's affairs had been put in order, had been deposited in a bank account for her needs in the future. But she didn't need to be told that she would not be able to live on that for the rest of her life. She needed to take matters into her own hands, and although Frederick might provide for her in the short term, she had no desire to be beholden to him further than that. Sitting at her small desk by the window of her room, she opened the box and unfolded her writing slope. Taking a sheet of the creamy writing paper and smoothing it flat, she picked up her nib pen in its silver holder and considered what to write.

LEONA J THOMAS

Madame Clapham's Modes *Dalton House*
1-2 Kingston Square, *Ackerby Road,*
Hull *Hull*

Dear Madam,
I am writing to enquire if there might be a position available for a seamstress within your esteemed emporium. I have been told that my stitching and embroidery skills are tolerably good and so hope that you might consider offering me a trainee position within your establishment.

Respectfully yours,
Kate E. Hoxton

CHAPTER EIGHTEEN

September 2018 York

After a few weeks it felt as if Kate have never been away from university. The new first-year students were now able to find their way around the campus and their initial new-found freedom had turned to acceptance that they were here to study. As a second-year student, Kate was continuing her English Literature and History course with resumed enthusiasm. She and Jen were back in the flat they had shared the previous year, courtesy of Jen's parents who let it out as an Airbnb out of term time. Jen was doing a completely different course so their paths rarely crossed within the university but, when they came home in the evenings, they would share the cooking or bring in a takeaway meal depending on how their funds were looking.

This evening Kate was on her own. Jen had made arrangements to go to the gym with some of her friends and then go on somewhere afterwards. Kate had some reading to do for her course and hoped to make a start on an essay that was due in at the end of the month. Before that, she wanted a quick check-in with Granny Sue.

Putting the phone on speaker, she chatted to Gran about what was going on here in York, while she shoved a microwave meal in to heat.

"What have you been up to this week Gran? Have you signed up for any new courses at the community centre?" she asked.

"In fact I have! I fancied Chinese for beginners but Sally wasn't up for it…"

"I'm not surprised!" chortled Kate.

"... so we decided to try Bookbinding and Papermaking Techniques on a Monday night – oh, and we're going to keep going with the Family History again," added Gran.

For some reason, Kate's stomach flipped with apprehension. She didn't really understand why but, having had some very strange experiences the last time she was in York, she felt that there had been a definite link with Gran's unearthing of the family's past.

Some other idle chit-chat filled the next few minutes before the microwave pinged and Gran said, "I'll let you get your supper then. Hope you're eating properly?"

"Of course! Love you Gran. Take care, hugs..."

Returning to her room after eating off a tray balanced on her lap, and watching a few minutes of some puerile soap, Kate slung the dishes in the sink for later and went back to her room where her notes were strewn on her bed. Shuffling them into some semblance of order, she opened up her laptop and sat back, thinking about where to start.

The old box sat further along the desk and she idly started running her fingers over the worn wood and the smooth brass keyhole.

*****

She unfolded the letter which had been delivered two days ago and read the short, but to the point, message again...

Dear Miss Hoxton,
Madame Clapham has asked me to inform you that she is requiring some young ladies to train in her establishment due to the phenomenal success of her business and increased custom from the ladies, not just in Hull, but from further afield in the county.

If you are able to attend on Monday next at 9am prompt, Madame

Clapham will be overseeing the possible hiring of some suitable young ladies. Please bring some examples of your work and be prepared to undertake a practical assessment.

Please reply by return to accept this invitation, and also send details of your full name, age and any previous experience.

Cecily Grainger,
Workroom manager

It was with some trepidation that she dressed in a black skirt and bodice and a white blouse with a starched white high-necked collar. Slipping her black fitted jacket on, she straightened the narrow cuffs at her wrists and tweaked the puffed tops at her shoulders. She had carefully folded some examples of her needlework skills – a nightgown with a smocked neck detail, a finely hemmed cambric petticoat, some embroidered handkerchiefs, an antimacassar with a crewelwork design and a lace-edged linen chemise, and these she laid carefully into a carpet bag, securing the strap and lifting it off the bed.

The household was still quiet and she wanted to be out before her aunt stirred or Frederick headed off to work. She had told Mrs Grimes that she would not require breakfast and to please not mention anything to her aunt, should she be missed, although her aunt usually took breakfast in her own room. She wished to arrive in plenty of time for her appointment at Madame Clapham's and soon was rattling along on the lower deck of the tram, brushing shoulders with other workers heading into the centre of town. The passengers were, in the main, clerks and junior businessmen, a few older ladies and some younger ladies looking like they had a bank or office position, and the odd workman in shabbier clothes, heading for the docks.

She arrived in the centre of town well ahead of her appointed time. She filled the time by strolling around the streets that led to Kingston Square. If any young ladies walked past her, headed towards the square, she wondered if perhaps they were also going to Madame Clapham's. How many would there be? She assumed there would be a few but was starting to feel a little intimidated as she headed back to the square and spied quite a few girls and young women starting to converge on the colonnaded front of the building. As the clock on the nearby church started to chime out 9 o'clock, a young lad in a bellboy uniform appeared from a side entrance to the building and spoke to the first girl in the queue and beckoned to the rest to follow. Rather than entering by the imposing front door, the group were led down the side of the building to an open door, which led into a basement area. Kate found herself in the middle of a group of about a dozen girls, some of whom were nervously chattering to their fellows while others looked pale and anxious. Kate definitely belonged to the latter. However, as the group descended the steps into the basement, a hush fell over them all and the clatter of the door closing behind them brought them to total silence.

Forward strode a woman with black hair, fiercely drawn back from her face and tightly wound into a bun at the nape of her neck. She had a long stick which she held vertically in front of her, more like a pointer than a walking cane, its brass ferrule tapping authoritatively on the floor to get their attention. She introduced herself as Miss Grainger. She explained that they were to each take a seat at one of the worktables and lay out the examples of their work which they had been asked to bring.

It seemed an age before she stopped by Kate's table and started to examine her work. She said nothing and gave little indication of whether it came up to her high standard, merely making some marks on the list of names she carried with her. Once she had completed her round of all the tables, she struck her stick twice on the stone floor to get their attention again. Reading from her list, she read out seven names. They should get their coats and leave quietly. They were not required. Thankfully Kate was not one of them. The remaining girls were asked to pack up their samples of work and then over the next few hours, they would be given some items to work on.

It was well into the early afternoon when Kate eventually walked out into the sunshine, holding in her hand a note informing her of the time she was to present herself at Madame Clapham's to begin her apprenticeship as one of the team of seamstresses and dressmakers. Her neck ached from bending over her stitching for the last few hours and her fingers were stiff and sore, but her heart was light and her footsteps fast as she headed towards the next part of her life.

*****

Kate massaged her hands and gazed at her fingers. No words stared out at her from the blank screen of her laptop. Her notes lay scattered where she had left them. The writing slope lay open and she pulled up the leather flap, fully expecting to see the creamy writing paper and folded letter from Madame Clapham's. But instead there was an empty void.

Kate felt unsteady and somewhat disorientated, but this feeling was becoming familiar and she realised she did not feel quite so shaken as she had on previous occasions. She was coming to terms with the fact that somehow, the past of her family and the present she inhabited had found a way to seamlessly cross over, using her as a channel. She did not know why, and it seemed to come unbidden, but very gradually she was becoming curious about her distant relatives' lives. Visiting the past was something a lot of people would give anything to be able to do. She wouldn't say she enjoyed the experience, but grudgingly she had to admit she found it intriguing. But she couldn't tell anyone – because she couldn't even begin to explain to herself how or why it happened.

CHAPTER NINETEEN

1894 Hull

Kate's days had settled into a rhythm, one of hard work and long hours, but she had learned to accept that this was her direction in life and she was soon to have to become independent. Much had happened over the previous months which was to completely disrupt the family's previously sedate and increasingly affluent life. Uncle Charles' business had collapsed, as a vast amount of compensation had to be paid due to the accident at the docks. Frederick carried the weight of blame as a heavy load which weighed him down, and he had visibly aged as a result, looking much older than his twenty-four years.

Each morning, Kate rose at six and by seven-thirty was on the tram into town. At eight o'clock precisely, she was admitted with the other girls to the basement of Madame Clapham's. Each girl had been given a brass ticket with their personal number stamped upon it. As they entered, they dropped the ticket into a box, to prove that they had started work on time. If they arrived a minute late, their wages were cut. They were often required to work late into the evening, often without any meal breaks – usually when there was a large or urgent order to complete. They were not described as trainees or apprentices; Madame Clapham insisted they referred to themselves as 'young ladies'. There were strict rules in the workrooms. They were not allowed to talk when working. Madame rarely came down to the workrooms but if she did, employees were not allowed to address her unless spoken to and were expected to remain busy at their work. Despite this, her 'young ladies' felt great pride and a sense of self-esteem from knowing that they were creating clothing for the salon's high-status clients. There was a marked contrast from the sparse workrooms, where her employees made the elaborate outfits, to the luxurious showrooms on the upper floors where the gowns were modelled and her customers were measured, fabrics were chosen and designs altered to fit her wealthy clientele.

Nevertheless, Kate would return home at the end of a long and often exhausting day with a sense of achievement. Her fingers were inevitably stiff from gripping the needle and her back and shoulders ached from being in one position for hours on end. But she was learning so much and even earning slight indications of praise from the indomitable Miss Grainger.

It was to prove a fortuitous decision to have taken employment at Madame Clapham's as, one evening as she returned to Dalton House, she was met in the hallway by Frederick who asked her to join him and her aunt in the drawing room. Aunt Eliza sat in her usual chair, seeming to have shrunk over the past few months, and still swathed in mourning clothes. She looked up as Kate entered and gave her a feeble smile. Sitting down on the couch as indicated by her cousin, she scanned their faces for a clue as to what was to come.

Frederick stood with his back to the fire, his hands clasped behind him, staring down and rocking on the balls of his feet, so like his father used to do. He cleared his throat and took a deep breath.

"Dear Kate, you are, of course, aware of what has befallen this family over the past few months although you may not have been party to all the details. It has proved far more devastating than we could have imagined. Not only has Father's business been crippled financially but the creditors have called in their debts and, to put it bluntly, we have had to use the remaining capital to pay off the shareholders and dissolve the company." Here he paused and Aunt Eliza's shoulders shook as she took a deep and shuddering breath, keeping her eyes downcast and focussed on her wedding ring, which she was rotating round and round her bony finger.

Kate looked up at him with a sense of foreboding as he continued, "To put it bluntly, dear cousin, we will have to sell Dalton House, as well as liquidating some other assets and selling various bonds and shares that father had purchased. This will only barely cover our debts."

Kate gasped and Aunt Eliza let out a little whimper, retrieved her handkerchief from her reticule and dabbed at her eyes. "I see," was all Kate could say.

"I don't think you do, my dear. Mother has decided to take up my sister Becky's offer to live with her and her husband in Leeds. I shall return to Leeds with them but I will need to try to obtain a position, which may prove difficult with my present … reputation. In fact, I may look to going abroad as I fear I will not be able to find anything suitable in this country where petty-minded people spread evil rumours far and wide!" Frederick's voice had risen and now he was striding about the room, his gruff tones visibly distressing his mother.

"Oh Frederick! Please don't say that…" Aunt Eliza's tremulous tones could be barely heard as she buried her face in her hands and stifled her sobs in the lacy folds of her handkerchief.

Kate went over to her aunt and knelt beside her, putting an arm around her quivering shoulders and feeling the bony edges through the shawl that she had wrapped around her.

Frederick continued, "So you see Kate, there will have to be a good many changes ahead. In a couple of weeks, you will have reached your eighteenth birthday and I will release the money Father had put in trust for you. I hope that you may be able to use it to help you plan your future. I know you have found a position in town, and I hope that it will give you some security in the short term. I am so sorry that I cannot be more optimistic."

"I quite understand," Kate replied quietly, her voice almost a whisper. Set adrift again, she thought to herself.

*****

The front door closed for the last time. The carts were loaded with the few bits of furniture and trunks that the family were taking with them. An auction was to be held the following week to sell off the rest of the household items to raise a little more cash. A hansom cab had pulled up and Frederick had helped his mother inside, wrapping a rug around her and arranging the few bags she would be taking with her in person on the train to Leeds.

Mrs Grimes stood on the doorstep, feebly waving her off, before picking up her bag and heading to catch a tram to take her to her new lodgings in the Groves, one of the poorer areas of Hull. Tears were evident in her eyes, as they had been in Aunt Eliza's as she had had to give her notice. Mrs Grimes had been with the family for over twenty years and it was a cruel wrench for her. Approaching sixty, she was unsure what employment she would be able to find, even though Aunt Eliza had placed advertisements in the 'Positions Sought' section of the newspapers for her, offering her services as a very experienced and reliable housekeeper. She fervently hoped that she would find a position soon. The two maids had been given notice and had already departed the previous week, hopefully to find work, as their references had been glowing.

And that left Kate…

CHAPTER TWENTY

1894-5 Hull

Once again, I felt as if I had been set adrift. Belonging to no-one. Nowhere to call home.

I found lodgings, the best I could afford on my meagre wages, a room in a court of buildings off Lime Street. It was far from what I'd been used to with the Atkinsons. My days took on a rhythm of their own; a walk over the bridge to Madame Clapham's to start work at eight, long hours hunched over my sewing, fingers stiff and sore, then a walk home as evening fell, pausing only to buy some basic items to eat upon my return. I grew thinner, and my clothes began to hang on me. At least I had the skills to alter them enough to hide where my bony shoulders showed through the fabric, and I usually made sure I had a shawl around me while sitting in the workroom – and not only to keep out the chill.

I slept badly, even though I was beyond tired. I knew I must look like a shadow of the young girl who had first accompanied Aunt Eliza to Madame Clapham's to order new gowns. How quickly things could change.

But I also became aware of a presence that insinuated itself into my mind, unbidden and unwelcome. I could not rid myself of it. It came most days as I walked to or from my work and at first, I could not make sense of where it emanated from. Then the memory of the insidious tones came back to me, and I realised that the last time I had heard it was the night of the dock collapse. Now it followed me, stalked me and haunted me. As I crossed the bridge over the sluggish muddy river, the stench of it filled my nostrils – and its presence filled my mind.

Good morning.
Nice to see you today.

You are trying to ignore me but I know you can hear me.

I have a message from an old acquaintance of yours.
It would love to see you again.

You look tired.
Come to me.
I can soothe you.

*****

Day after interminable day…

Months have passed. I cannot bear it. Should I challenge it, or give in to it? I have tried going another, longer way back to my room. I avoid the bridges, the docks, the sewers that run into it – any link with it, but it finds me. It always finds me…

I was called into Miss Grainger's office this morning. Her face was thunderous as she stood to address me.

"Miss Hoxton, I fear your work is falling far below what is expected of you. You have been late twice in the last fortnight and there are times when you look as if you are almost asleep at your workbench. You will have to buck up your ideas or else we shall be forced to give you notice. Take this as your last warning."

I stood, stunned, for a few moments before she sniffed, "You may go!"

*****

I was eventually dismissed from Madame Clapham's. I was so sad to have to leave as, at one time, it had seemed the answer to all my prayers and presaged such a new start for me.

*Come nearer, little one.
I can soothe your cares away.*

It would have been so easy just to follow the sound and ease away all my troubles. But then it occurred to me that *it* was the cause of them. I had to escape from its stifling influence. That night, as I pulled the worn blanket over me and tried to find some ease upon the thin mattress that was my bed, I considered my options. Images from my past swirled through my exhausted mind, tired of trying, tired of fighting. Happier times when we were a family, altogether in our cosy home on Lowther Street in York. Waiting for Papa to return from a trip with a treat for Henry and me. The warm smell of newly baked bread in our little kitchen, Mama laying it on the wooden table and slicing off a piece of the crust and handing it to me. I could see the butter oozing and melting into the soft dough and hurried to wrap my mouth around it, before it oozed between my fingers. Papa carrying me up to bed when I fell asleep on his knee, laying me softly on my little bed and covering me gently with the quilt. He would whisper 'Night night little 'un, sleep tight' under his breath, fearing to wake me, but I would always whisper back, 'an' don't let the bugs bite.' And now they were all gone – every one of them.

What had it said?

*I have a message from an old acquaintance of yours.
It would love to see you again.*

Who did I know?
Where?

*****

I shall not tell you how low I fell. I am ashamed. I knew I had to do something to escape the prison my mind was making for me, but I didn't know how. How long I could have gone on like that,

I cannot say, but it was a chance meeting with Mrs Grimes that was my salvation.

I was standing by the doorway of one of the many public houses, what for I do not really know, when I heard a voice calling my name. "Miss Hoxton, Kate, is that you?"

I could barely lift my head to look in its direction. Wisps of my hair had escaped my bonnet and straggled into my eyes. As I brushed them off my face, I saw a familiar rotund figure in front of me.

"Surely it can't be Miss Kate!" the voice continued, sounding both shocked and distraught.

Squinting, I began to discern familiar features to go with the voice. "Mrs Grimes?" I muttered, as an overwhelming mix of shame and recognition came over me. My legs gave way beneath me and the last thing I saw was the cobbles rushing up to meet me.

The softness of the pillow beneath my head and the warmth of the covers that were draped over me brought me such comfort that I didn't want to open my eyes for a few moments. When I did, it was dear Mrs Grimes' face looking down at me, her hand gently patting mine as she made tutting noises. I let myself slip away again to a place where I didn't have to think, or listen, or try to escape.

*****

I stayed with Mrs Grimes, in her simple lodgings, until I felt much improved. She fed me up and fussed over me, bringing back wholesome food to cook each evening after she finished her work as a washerwoman. Having spent the day up to her elbows in water, she would dry and fold the linens and deliver them to her customers by the time it got dark. If they weren't dry, she would drape them around the room on a pulley or wooden frame near the small range, hoping that a night inside would render them ready for delivery the following day.

What little she had, she shared with me, refusing my protestations about being a burden to her. When I felt more recovered, I was able to lend a hand with the laundry and between us we were often able to complete the work in almost half the time. I felt I owed her so much, I couldn't begin to thank her, but when I broached the subject, she always brushed aside my comments, "Cum lass, what else would 'ah 'ave done for 'ee?"

But as the weeks went on, I knew I had to make plans for the future. This town had nothing for me, and I needed to leave it far behind with all its associations and bad memories. I could not continue to be dependent on Mrs Grimes. I was saddened that she had not found a position more suited to her, but she merely shrugged and said at least she had found something.

My thoughts returned to the only time I could recall feeling warmth and comfort. That was when we lived as a family in York. Why I felt that things would be better there, I don't know. If only I could have seen what was ahead.

Mrs Grimes pushed a few shillings of her hard-earned savings into my hand and all but pushed me into the third-class carriage of the York train. Handing me up my small bag and the only other possession I had, my writing slope box, she leant forward and held my hands in her rough ones and said, "God go wi' ye, lass. Ah wish ye well. Mind, ah'm allus 'ere if ye need me." With that she turned away, but not before I could see the glint of tears in her eyes. The guard slammed the door shut and as the whistle blew and the train shuddered into motion, the last sight I had of her was bustling down the platform, her shawl held up to her face.

CHAPTER TWENTY-ONE

November 1900 York

Hindsight is a wonderful thing, so they say, and had Kate Eliza Hoxton known what was ahead of her, perhaps she might have headed to anywhere else but York – Leeds, Lincoln, Wakefield, anywhere but where her feet and her heart had taken her. A mistaken belief that returning to a well-loved place will bring back those warm feelings and the sense of contentment which were once experienced there. Five or more years had passed, and all she had found was the daily grind of keeping yourself barely above the poverty line. Earning enough to pay your rent and have a pittance left to put by for 'a rainy day' – which seemed to come more often than it should.

Ma Simpson, her landlady, by day euphemistically called herself 'a laundress' but in the darker hours, she organised her 'ladies' from the back room that led out onto the dark lane that ran down the side of the red brick terrace into a squalid yard. Upstairs, she let out rooms to those who could pay and keep the rent coming regularly. Downstairs, she rented out rooms for a different purpose and offered them rent-free for those who could no longer find the few shillings required to keep themselves in their private rooms upstairs. That was the choice she offered them. Either way, they had a roof over their head. Otherwise, their only other choice was the door to the street.

Kate might tell you that she tried to blot out the muffled sounds from below. She might tell you that thankfully another week had passed when she had had enough to pay the rent and could remain upstairs in her shared room. She might tell you that she collapsed thankfully on to her thin mattress in her small upstairs room she shared with Annie Benson, turning down the gaslight after they had both completed the garments they had been stitching. Like Kate, Annie was a dressmaker, though her talents were lesser than Kate's and so she undertook hemming and mending, rather than making and altering. Kate's apprenticeship with Madame Clapham had stood her in good stead and she had a regular clientele – if it could be called as such, her reputation and skill being spread by word of mouth – the best form of advertising, and the cheapest.

Nevertheless, she was still bound by her past and bouts of 'melancholy', as the doctor called them. When the dark thoughts came to her, when she might shout out in her sleep, when she would be heard talking to invisible voices, then she would be afraid to leave her room. Her work went unfinished, the orders unfulfilled. And inevitably, she would find herself on the street, looking for a refuge until she regained her equilibrium.

Over the years there had been several of these episodes, each time clearer and stronger. But she met them with more fortitude, the reassurance that they would pass giving her the strength to endure them. She knew the warning signs. She felt the presence. She steeled her resolve not to give in this time. And so far, she had managed to come out the other side, not always aware of what had passed in the dark hours – days? – in between.

Ma Simpson was always there to take her in, always with an eye to 'business' as Kate was a pretty thing, those clear eyes very beguiling and her 'visitors' would be sure to appreciate being captivated by them. But, so far, Kate had refused any such arrangement. But time would tell, Ma Simpson would call after her, "Time will tell, my girl!"

*****

York is a city well known for its floods. The Yorkshire Ouse is a capricious river, at times peaceful and welcoming, bringing raw materials and people from the south and taking the goods made there to be traded far and wide. It has ever been so. For centuries.

And for centuries, it has also been known for the times it floods, when it inundates the low-lying parts of the city, the quaysides – staithes as they are known locally, the lanes and alleys that run up from the banks, the public houses and warehouses that cluster by the edges, the hovels of the poorest folk who scratch a living in that city.

As the year that marked the first of the new decade was drawing to a close, the autumn gales blew in and squalls of heavy rain blew in from the south-west. The skies were dark and gloomy for days and with them, Kate's mood. She knew the signs, she felt the quivering in her legs as she walked the narrow alleys and cobbled streets, visiting her customers and struggling with the bundles of clothing to be altered, or fabric to be cut and shaped to approximate the latest fashion. Except, with her customers, the latest fashion had already been superseded by another trend. Her customers were the ones who aimed for respectability but didn't quite make it to the ranks of those who could peruse the latest catalogues and magazines showing the newly arrived modes from Paris, or the latest styles worn at court in the capital. But try they did, and thankfully they sought her out. She didn't have a business card, or headed notepaper, or a regular advertisement in the Yorkshire Gazette, but her clients found her and personal recommendations kept her well supplied with customers.

Having delivered her order to one of her regular ladies who lived in the Crescent, off Blossom Street, she made her way back, hugging the shelter of the old city walls and tying her bonnet strings as tightly as she could, her umbrella of no use in the gusty wind. The Skeldergate Bridge stretched ahead of her, the bare trees at the side thrashing in the gale that whipped up the river. The few people who were crossing ahead of her were skittering along, skirts tangling around their legs and hats clamped firmly to heads. But as she bowed her head into the wind and made to set forth across the open pavement, the low monotone overcame the whistling and roaring of the wind.

> *Always a pleasure to see you again.*
> *Isn't this fun?*
> *The fierceness, the power, the strength I have.*
> *But you know that already…*

She tried stopping up her ears, but the insidious voice was not silenced. It permeated her thoughts and was not modulated by the whistling of the wind, the spattering of the rain or the pressure of her gloved hands upon her ears.

> *You know you want to renew our friendship.*
> *It's been a while.*
> *After all, you are mine.*
> *Your mother and I were – shall we say … acquainted.*
> *Family, that's what we are…*

Someone watching her progress would have either put her lurching gait and unsteady progress down to the force of the gale, or perhaps even assumed she had been imbibing something intoxicating, especially if they were to hear the low conversation held under her breath. As it was, no-one gave her a second glance, too focussed in getting themselves out of the storm and into the shelter of a cosy room. The clouds had already darkened beyond the evening's usual gloom, now turning more ominous by the minute. But Kate was wrapped in her own darkness, her own cloak of invisibility. She neither saw where she went, nor was seen to fade into the ever-deepening obscurity of that dreadful night.

*****

The headlines in the local newspaper the following days told of inundated homes and businesses, boats snatched from moorings, trees uprooted and being tossed around in the fast-flowing water, the arches under bridges choked with the flotsam being washed downstream. And also the unfortunates who had found themselves caught by the flood – a few to be plucked out of the murky waters just in time, but others only discovered too late in the tangle of wreckage and rubbish accumulating at the edges of the staithes.

She was told later that she was one of the latter, assumed drowned and beyond help, but miraculously when her limp form was dragged out and laid on the cobbles, someone spotted the merest flicker of an eye, the ghost of a breath. She had been carried somewhat unceremoniously to a nearby church, the most convenient place to lay her down and call for aid.

Hours passed before she was able to give her name and her dwelling place. By that time, she had been administered to by the local cleric's wife, given a warm place to lie in their home and dry clothes to replace her sodden, muddied ones. The darkness lifted from her, but the memory of last hours – was it even days? Nothing seemed to come, however hard she tried to piece together the shattered scraps that flitted through her mind like dark velvet moths, just beyond seeing, never close enough to grasp or be able to fix an image or an outline.

You came to me at last.
What a dance we had.
Holding you close, closer still.
Then I made you mine.
We are one, you and I.
I knew I would possess you one day – just like those who went before...

The cleric's wife kindly accompanied her back to Ma Simpson's and fussed over her, wanting to make sure that she was well enough to return. Her landlady did not welcome the visitation of a woman of the church but rose to the occasion and feigned her overwhelming concern for the poor girl, assuring the woman that she would be more than able to escort Kate inside and take care of her needs for the foreseeable future; it was after all, her Christian duty so to do. Almost pushing her aside, she shut the door firmly and stood, hands on hips, appraising the dishevelled creature in her hallway. Kate merely held up her hand, pre-empting the flood of invective that was sure to follow, and headed for the stairs and the sanctuary of her room.

The words that followed her did nothing to cheer her, "And yer behind wi' yer rent!"

*****

On the evening of Sunday, 31 March 1901, Ma Simpson recorded those who were in her abode on census night. That is to say, she circumspectly noted those who usually resided at her abode each and every night, not just those present on that particular night. To have done otherwise would have compromised both her reputation, such as it was, and those of her 'guests'. When the enumerator came to call and collect the census form, duly completed by the head of the household, on the Monday afternoon, he scrutinised it, noted that all the information had been accurately entered in the relevant boxes, and wearily left to rap on the next door and repeat this performance throughout his allotted area.

And so who are we to think otherwise? That is what history has recorded and they are the facts. But are they the *true* facts? Kate might tell you differently. She might tell you that they had no idea what Ma Simpson had entered on the census form; all she had asked of them was where they had been born. If they didn't know for sure, she entered an approximation. Four residents in that house in Caistor Street. Respectable women, you might surmise, from the occupations and situation. But Kate knew that she would very soon have to make alternative arrangements. Whatever had resulted on that stormy night had given rise to a new life that was making itself felt inside her. There was a gnawing feeling that flitted over her, at times causing her to shiver involuntarily but at other times, she felt almost a warmth and sense of being secure, held in the arms of one whose only concern was her comfort and pleasure. Such an alien feeling, one she had never experienced since a young child. But the outcome was unmistakable, as well as bewildering. She tried to unravel the tangled shreds of memories but, mercifully, she could not. She could only assume she had suffered some form of assault in the dark hours of her oblivion. Soon she would not be able to hide the outcome from either her clients, or her landlady.

But women like Ma Simpson were far shrewder than Kate gave her credit for, and it was only a few days later that she cornered her in the hallway and beckoned her into the downstairs parlour, quiet and empty at this time of day.

" 'Ow far gone?" she barked without any preamble. Kate was taken aback, not only with the harshness of the question, but by the fact that she had hoped that what she had suspected might be an error, a mistake, certainly not a reality.

Seeing Kate visibly paling before her, she continued, "Well, it's 'appened afore, and it'll 'appen again. Ye can stay 'ere as long as 'ee can pay rent, t'otherwise ye knows what'll 'appen. An' there's allus another kind 'o work for 'ee, if ye want it – later."

"I will keep paying what I owe – as long as I am able," Kate replied, her voice tremulous and barely audible.

"Aye, well, we'll see..." was the only response. Then as an afterthought she added, "An' this 'ere letter came for 'ee earlier." She held out the small, folded missive and Kate could see the bold, heavily imprinted handwriting upon it. Taking it, she headed up to her room, mercifully unoccupied by her roommate, and sat down on her bed, lifting the writing box onto her knee and opening it to retrieve a small paper knife with which to break the red wax seal.

CHAPTER TWENTY-TWO

October 2018 Lincoln

Gran dug out the folder from between the pile of papers and magazines which had accumulated on the side table beside the television over the past few months. The pile threatened to tumble onto the floor, as Gran balanced the leaning tower with her knee and winkled out the notes from the Family History course she had attended the previous session. It finally gave in to gravity, and the rest of the stack slid haphazardly onto the floor, spilling across the brightly coloured rug, and bringing forth some choice words from Gran. Having laid the folder aside, she spent the next few minutes sorting the random selection of periodicals and old newspapers into 'keep', 'recycle' and 'make my mind up later about you' piles. Finally, she was able to flop onto the couch and lay the folder on her knee.

It was months since she had last looked at it, in fact probably the last time was when Kate came home from Uni in June and she had shown her what research she had done so far and laid out the evidence of their previous generations. She needed to refresh her mind about where she had got up to and skim over the tutor's notes in preparation for the upcoming evening class later this week. Her friend Sally had romped ahead now with her research, having done her DNA, discovered a missing branch of her family and been in regular email contact with a distant cousin in Australia. As a result, she had decided not to enrol in this term's Family History class and had opted for 'Pastel Drawing for Beginners' instead. "Been there, done that," was Gran's response when Sally sought out her company, so it was just Gran herself returning this term.

She couldn't believe how much she had forgotten and, after the best part of an hour revisiting her tutor's notes followed by her own research, she felt she owed herself a cuppa and a chocolate brownie, freshly baked that morning in readiness for the WI meeting that evening.

Balancing a cup of herbal tea on the now, almost empty side table, she turned back to the certificates she had sent for and the printed-out sheets with the census, newspaper reports and other information upon them. Where to begin? What little puzzle was there to start another line of enquiry?

Her eye fell on the 1901 census, the copy of which she had printed out from the Ancestry image she had discovered online. Kate Eliza Hoxton, her great grandmother, seemed to be flipping backwards and forwards between York and Hull. Why? Born in 1876 in York, mother Laura, father, William Hoxton. In 1881 still there in Lowther Street with her parents and older half-brother Henry. But then in 1891 in Hull with her aunt and uncle. She was momentarily puzzled, but then recalled the awful tragedy that had befallen the family. The drownings at Naburn Lock in 1882 had been reported in the newspaper, and here was the printout from the Yorkshire Gazette at the time.

A woman and her child were drowned near Naburn Lock last week. Every effort was made to recover the bodies but in vain until Thursday last due to the extreme flood conditions when the child was found and taken out of the river at Acaster Malbis. An inquest was held at Naburn yesterday when a waterman gave evidence that the alarm was given when the child fell overboard. On asking the little daughter how her brother had fallen in, she said he tipped over after standing on the side and then her mother had jumped in to save him. This is doubly heart-breaking for the child as the boat was returning the body of Mr Hoxton, a well-known and respected waterman and coal merchant and the husband of the family, for burial in York after his passing in Hull the previous week. Verdict : 'Accidentally drowned.' The body of the mother has not yet been found.

Yorkshire Gazette 15 Dec 1882

So ... here was the conundrum. What had happened in the intervening years? How had Kate Eliza found herself back in York in 1901, on her own, no sign of her aunt and uncle, living in Caistor Road, York, and working as a dressmaker?

Gran sat back and sipped thoughtfully at her herbal tea, dropping the sodden bag on the plate beside her half-eaten chocolate brownie. Her imagination could conjure up a selection of possibilities. But there would be a slim possibility of verifying any of them, as there would be little or no paper trail to unearth. History is only built on the facts that survive. The rest is merely conjecture, imagined by those who seek to fill in the gaps.

She looked again at the 1901 census information.

Caistor Street								
	Mary Simpson	Head	W	53	Laundress	Own account	At home	Yorks, York
	Anne C. Benson	Boarder	S	26	Dressmaker	"	"	Yorks, Driffield
	Kate E. Hoxton	Boarder	S	24	Dressmaker	"	"	Yorks, York
	Doris E. Williams	Boarder	S	23	Laundress	"	"	Yorks, York

What she could do was check if Caistor Street still existed on the modern street map of York.

But what the census did not record was perhaps the most important fact of all...

CHAPTER TWENTY-THREE

2018 York

For the first time, Kate made a conscious decision to try to link to her namesake from over a century before. Half the time she thought she was crazy; she certainly couldn't tell anyone or they would say she was *definitely* crazy! At other times, she felt such a link to her ancestor, a closeness and an empathy that was quite overwhelming. It was as if they were one. The writing slope had become a fascination, almost an obsession, and she had begun to delve deeper into their history and development. One of the tutors told them that one of the optional modules focussed on independent research work related to an artefact of their choice. They were to work on it it over the next few months, then deliver their research to their fellow students as a presentation. Immediately Kate was sure what the focus of her research would be.

But how many of her fellow students would be able to *see* their chosen artefacts and handle them in the past!

In the quiet of her bedroom in the flat, Kate tried to focus her mind on her namesake. As yet, she had not mastered how to make the link, as it usually came unbidden and without warning, but she thought that perhaps opening her mind, and being more receptive would enable the process – whatever that was.

Nothing. She took a deep breath and closed her eyes, running her fingertips over the smooth wooden edges of the writing slope. She tried saying Kate's name silently in her mind. Still nothing. She opened the slope and let her hands follow the joints and edges, the smooth, worn leather and the scooped-out compartments. Letting out a long breath, she sat back and stared at the hand in which she held the cockle shell ...

*****

With shaking hands, she unfolded the letter that Ma Simpson had given her, the stiff paper letting out a quiet crackle as the folds fought back against their enforced creases. The words were few and to the point, and her eyes flew first to the signature, before returning to the words themselves. It was from her cousin Frederick and, he regretted to inform her, her Aunt Eliza had passed away at the end of the previous week, while still living with her daughter in Leeds. It had been a short but debilitating illness, and she had mercifully passed peacefully at the end. The funeral was to be held the day after tomorrow – did she wish to attend?

The tears came quickly and her heart ached at the thought of dear Aunt Eliza having left this world in pain. She felt that her aunt never really got over the shock of losing Uncle Charles and the reduction in their means and standing after his business was so badly affected after the dock accident. She wondered if she should offer some excuse for not attending, her mind racing about whether she would be able to hide the small swelling of her belly. But heavy winter clothes should remedy that and she could easily make some alterations to her black outfit, should that be necessary. Her mind made up, she hastily penned a reply, offering her condolences and confirming that she would take the train to Leeds early on the morning of the funeral, which was to be held in the afternoon, and she would take the returning train late that evening. Her work commitments necessitated her return immediately, she explained further.

*****

The funeral had been a sad affair, as was to be expected and the women returned to her cousin Becky's home, while the men accompanied the cortege to the cemetery and laid her aunt to rest. Later that evening, as Frederick accompanied her in the cab to the station, he broke the news to her that he had decided to emigrate to South Africa, where he had been assured that his engineering skills would be put to good use. Having never been particularly close to Becky, Kate felt that her last relative was deserting her and, as she sat in the carriage as it had rattled and lurched back to York, she felt truly alone.

The following Sunday, she attended church as usual, and as she sat on the hard unforgiving pew, she offered up a prayer for her aunt's soul, and gave thanks to the Lord for her kindness and charity in taking her in, all those years before.

Her emotions threatened to overwhelm her when they rose to sing a hymn, and she reached forward to grasp the rail in front of her to steady herself. Next to her a young boy of about five or six years old turned to look up at her, and beside him stood a man, his father she presumed, turning the pages of the hymnal, and squinting at the small print. The man nudged the lad, and frowned at the boy's rudeness, urging him to look ahead and try to sing some of the words of the hymn. Kate looked away and surreptitiously dabbed at her eyes under her black veil, as she now wore a mourning outfit. But when the hymn was over and the reverend indicated they should sit, the boy looked back up at her with undisguised curiosity. This brought forth an even more forceful nudge from his father.

As the congregation filed out of the small church, to the shuffling of feet and muted conversations, Kate felt a hand upon her arm and turning round saw the same young lad who had filed out of the pew in her wake. He said nothing, but merely smiled up at her sadly, as if to ascertain the cause of her sorrow. By the time they had reached the door of the church and they could feel the shaft of cold air whipping round the archway, the boy's father had moved forward and left the church at her side.

"A'm reet sorry for ma lad's impertinence. Ah'd give him a clout if t'weren't for us being in't church!"

"Please, don't! He was merely sensing something in me and felt he had to show his sympathy."

"See Da, she's naw angry," the boy piped up, before being shushed again by his father.

"What's his name?" Kate asked.

"Ah'm James," the boy interjected before his father could reply, "Ah'm nearly six, and ma wee brother, ee's nearly two. Ee's called Amos."

At this, his father took him firmly by the arm, causing the lad to wince with the strength of the grasp.

"Ah can only apologise again, Miss," the man reiterated.

"It's of no consequence, Mr …?" Kate tried to mollify him.

"Davis, Miss. We'll be on our way, an' no cause ye any more offence."

"None was taken Mr Davis. In fact, young James here has made me smile, and I don't feel I've done that for some time. Thank you, James."

At this, James drew himself tall and looked at his father as if to say, "See!"

A blast of chilly air whipped the last of the fallen leaves and had a few of the early daffodils flaunting their half open blooms as if to presage the coming of spring around the corner.

"Which way are you goin' home? We can walk wi' ye if ye like?" young James piped up, earning him another frown from his father.

"I'd like that, James. We can walk some of the way together if you like," Kate smiled down at the boy. "Don't apologise again, Mr Davis – I can see you were about to. I'd be glad of a little company."

And so the course of history was changed by the simple actions of a child. Kate was not to know, but with the benefit of the scant records that map out the stepping-stones of history, we can see that the future was changing course for her.

*****

Kate was relieved to find that this revelation was not one of pain or sorrow occurring in her ancestor's past. And for a few moments she found herself smiling and looking down at young James, but his image faded as the door slammed and Jen's voice ran out, "Hi Kate, I'm back! I brought us a Chinese takeaway. You hungry? I'm starving!" And with that she was brought back to the present with a jolt.

CHAPTER TWENTY-FOUR

1901 York

As the months passed, miraculously Kate suffered no more 'bouts of melancholy' as the doctor had named them. But her mind was constantly in a state of turmoil. The only saving grace was that Ma Simpson had allowed her to remain in her lodging but she had had to decline orders from some of her customers, at least those who might take offence at her state, being an unmarried woman. She still had some who sent their orders through a maid, and she managed to get some work repairing and making up overalls for the workers at the local chocolate factory.

She found herself looking forward to seeing young James and his father each Sunday, and James always pushed his way ahead of the crowd to secure a seat for himself and his father on the same pew. But her condition was starting to become obvious, no matter how she tried to alter her garments, and she was conscious of some stares and whispered conversations as people stood around outside after the service.

Eventually she plucked up the courage to address Mr Davis. "I fear that I will not be able to attend church for a while."

"Are you goin' away?" piped up James.

"Something like that," she blushed at the lie and hoped his father didn't notice.

"Ah'll miss 'ee," he responded.

"An' so will ah," added Mr Davis, shaking his head and looking away as if he couldn't believe he had just said that.

"Thank you, that is very kind of you – both," she answered

quietly.

"We'll walk back wi' ye aways. Can we go through the park Da?" James asked, already racing ahead.

Kate would rather have made a discreet departure but instead, found herself in the company of the duo and many others who were enjoying the early spring sunshine and walking by the river through St George's Field.

"How is your other little boy, Mr Davis – Amos isn't it?" asked Kate.

"Well 'ee's grand, thanks for askin'. 'Ee's only just turned two but 'ee chatters away like a good 'un," Mr Davies replied.

"Does your wife not come along with you both and the little lad when you come to church? I hope you don't think it impertinent of me asking," she added hastily.

"She passed away – near two years since. Ah leave the lad wi' me landlady. She goes t' evenin' service an' so the arrangement suits us both."

"I am so sorry to hear of the loss of your wife. It must be very hard for you to have the two boys to raise yourself."

"Ah think ye have lost summun close, by yer dress," he nodded, taking in her mourning clothes which she always wore.

It would have been so easy for her to answer truthfully and talk about her dear Aunt, who had departed this world but a few months earlier. Instead she hesitated, just for a few moments, as wild thoughts went through her mind and she could almost perceive a plan, a way out of the worrisome months that loomed ahead. Ahead of them an older couple stood and vacated one of the benches that edged the walkway, under the trees now in blossom. He indicated that they should sit, and she gratefully accepted.

In barely a whisper she replied, "My situation is far worse than you can imagine, Mr Davis," and in a rush, before she could think better of it, she spun a story, a lie, but one to mitigate the situation she found herself in. "I was betrothed to – a sailor, and we were all but married. The banns were called and we had already taken rent on a little place to call our own. Then he drowned, a terrible accident at the docks, in Hull…"

At this, she dabbed at her eyes with an embroidered handkerchief which she withdrew from her jacket pocket, shocking herself with the ease of weaving such a falsehood.

"Ah'm reet sorry for 'ee, lass. That must 'ave been a terrible shock for 'ee. 'Ave ye no family to take ye in?"

"No, I fear I am alone in this world. My closest relative, a distant cousin, is by now probably halfway across the ocean headed for South Africa." She hesitated. Should she confront him with the biggest lie of all? As she paused, he took her hand and gave it a squeeze, by way of commiseration and perhaps, finding a kindred spirit. "Now you will think very badly of me. I fear you will be shocked by my situation." She hesitated again, using the pause to meet his eyes and fix them with her gaze, holding them there just long enough to note the effect that they had upon him. "I am with child…" She broke the gaze and looked down in shame, uttering the merest sob and withdrawing her hand from his.

Long minutes passed and it seemed that he would make no response. She had dealt the cards, now she would have to watch them play out.

"Ah see. An' ye would 'ave married 'im an' been a family soon enough," a statement of fact, not a question.

"Yes, that's it exactly. Our babe would have been born almost nine months from the date of our planned wedding. But it was not to be. And now…" She allowed herself another sob, but this time it came from the heart for there was no going back, and by saying it aloud, she had allowed herself to believe it. This *was* her situation. This *was* how it would be. She would be a single woman with a child, alone in the world. Not the first, not the last.

"And now, Mr Davis, I fear our – acquaintance – must come to an end. I shall have to go away soon, as you will appreciate. My landlady has already discovered my secret and I am threatened with eviction when the time comes that I can no longer keep myself and the child and earn money for the rent."

She made to stand but was interrupted by the arrival of James who had been throwing stones into the river. "Da, Da! Did tha' see? Did tha' see 'ow far I can throw 'em?"

"Aye, lad," he replied, distractedly. "Well done…"

Seeing Kate beginning to stand, he whined, "Aw no, we don't 'ave t'go, do we?"

Mr Davis pressed his hand upon her arm and indicated that she should stay. "Tha' don't need t'go, lass. Sit awhile longer. 'Tis good for the lad t' get the fresh air. 'An I can tell 'ee a bit about me'sen." After the briefest hesitation as she tried to protest, she resumed her seat and the lad ran off, exhorting them to watch him again.

"Tha' situation ain't so far away from me own. Me wife, Franny, was in't family way wi' our child on the day we were wed. We loved each other very much, an', well, tha' knows 'ow that is…" He reddened and turned away for a moment or two. "James were born a few months later, an' then she lost one – a girl t'was – she only lived for a day. But then she 'ad young Amos near four years after James. She took ill almost straightway after 'is birth. She never lasted t'week. T'were touch an' go wi' Amos, but 'e survived an' I thank the good Lord for him every day. 'e's the spit of his Ma, God rest 'er soul." He paused for breath, not used to making such long speeches.

"I am so sorry to hear that Mr Davis. We are indeed, poor souls thrown upon the mercy of the world. And thank you for being so kind to show me such compassion, in my circumstances. Now I really must be heading back. I have sewing to complete for delivery tomorrow morning."

They stood and made to head back, and young James soon came running up to join them. As they parted ways, Mr Davis halted for a moment and said quietly, "Ah hope we will see you again soon. Mebbe I could call on ye sometime?" And with that, they went their separate ways.

*****

Having decided that she should soon stop attending church, and accordingly, stop meeting young James and Mr Davis, instead she found herself there the following Sunday and, once more, they enjoyed a saunter along by the river in the spring sunshine. And once more, Mr Davis indicated that they should sit awhile.

"If 'ee will allow me – ah'd like to suggest a proposition. Ah realise ah'm in no position to offer much, but …" and here he seemed to run out of words. She turned to face him directly, by way of encouraging him to continue. "Well," he faltered, "James 'as taken a reet like to ye, an' if ye pardon me saying so, so 'ave I." At this he reddened and turned away so she might not see his blushes. "Ah've not much t'offer," he continued, as he pressed on with the little speech he had been practising over the last few days, "but ah could put a roof over yer head an' a place to have the bairn. An' in return, mebbe ye'd be happy to care for the lads an' ah can get more time for work."

"I see, Mr Davis, so what you are proposing is … a housekeeper position, shall we say?"

"Well, ah suppose that's what ah'm suggesting. Nothing

improper, ah assure ye," he added hastily.

"And your landlady? How would she see this – arrangement?" Kate ventured.

"Well, the house but one is comin' up vacant an' it 'as an extra room. Tha'd 'ave yer own room, of course, see?" he added quickly.

"I think we understand each other Mr Davis. Would I be correct in assuming that what I would earn from my dressmaking would be added to your income and we could therefore pay the rent required?" This was met from a nod, and a relieved half smile. "Would it not seem improper for your reputation, never mind my own, to be living under the same roof?"

"Let people think what they like. 'Tis our business an' none of their's. But if ye feel ah'm takin' too many liberties, ah' am reet sorry an' apologise," he mumbled, wringing his hands, and looking at his feet.

Kate stood, rearranged her skirts and pulled her gloves tight. "You realise I shall have to consider this matter, Mr Davis. May I speak with you again next Sunday?"

Jumping to his feet, he assured her that of course, it was only right and proper that she should do so.

"By the way, I do not know your Christian name, Mr Davis. May I enquire it?" she asked as they started walking back the way they had come.

"Ah'm called Herbert, but everyone jus' calls me Bert."

"And I am Kate, Kate Hoxton. Let me use the coming days to consider your proposal, Mr Davis, and I shall give you my response next Sunday, if that suits you?"

And that is how they left it. But of course, Kate knew that this was a heaven-sent answer to her predicament. She would be away from the local neighbours who knew her, much that they would probably care, and she would have some security and still be able to pay her way and maintain some independence. Quite what Herbert's neighbours might think was another matter. No doubt, he would repeat the story about her pregnancy and the fact that she was 'a widow'. And this would probably ensure some semblance of respectability.

But there lingered in her some shreds of shame and guilt about her lies. But then again, what other choice did she have?

CHAPTER TWENTY-FIVE

October 2018 Lincoln

Granny Sue ran from the car, slamming the door behind her and holding her folder over her head as the rain came down in sheets, blown by the autumnal gale that swept across the flat lands of Lincoln. She had just attended the first Family History evening class of the new term. The same tutor was there and a few familiar faces who, like her, were returning to further their knowledge and hone their researching skills. But there were also a few new faces, and much of the class was taken up with a resume of where people were up to in their research, and what they were still looking for.

She had managed to get her folder into some semblance of order by generation, subdivided into date order with the various records she had located, interspersed with the actual certificates she had ordered. She had also uploaded her tree onto Ancestry and made a copy of it as a printout. Fortunately it did not yet cover more than two pages, unlike the man next to her, whose tree covered his desk and stretched beyond that onto a second one, before flopping off the end. Sue couldn't imagine what more he could hope to find! As it was, she had only got back to her two times great grandmother, Laura Harrison.

Having not looked at her folder for a few months, she needed to take some time to re-evaluate where she was up to and what her next steps would be. By the time she got home, she had noted down that she needed to send for Laura's birth certificate, the details of which she had located on Free BMD. She had been born in the Sculcoates area of Hull in the December quarter of 1843. She also wanted to find her on the 1861 and 1851 censuses. And she also wanted to find out more about Laura's daughter, Kate

Eliza Hoxton, Sue's great grandmother, who she had located in York on the 1901 census working as a dressmaker.

But first, she needed a strong cup of coffee – and a large slice of that chocolate cake would go down a treat. Shaking the raindrops off her jacket and leaving her sodden shoes in the hall, she went through to the cosy kitchen, still faintly smelling of the shepherd's pie she had eaten at dinner time. Ten minutes later she was snuggled up on the couch, clutching a hot mug of coffee in her hands and looking at the page of notes she had made earlier that evening. The wind rattled the loose casement window frames of the cottage but the thick curtains she had already drawn before leaving earlier were combatting most of the draughts.

Snuggled up next to her was a small black and white cat, Rosie, that had turned up at her door as a stray a couple of weeks ago and now had officially adopted Sue. Sue smiled, feeling that coming home to those gentle purrs was very welcoming. Now that her granddaughter was back in York, the house seemed very quiet again. Sue wondered what Kate might be doing on this stormy night. And then her thoughts turned to tracking down another Kate, Sue's great grandmother, who had returned to York and was down on the 1901 census as a dressmaker.

She laid down her now empty mug and pulled over her laptop. Having located the information she needed in her folder she resumed her search. This time she needed to find out what happened over the next few years to Kate and try and fill in some of the blanks. For example, Sue wondered why Kate had gone back to York when previously, she had been with her aunt, living comfortably in Hull. There are definitely intriguing gaps in history that we strain to fill, sometimes with our own imaginary possibilities, Sue mused. If only she had a crystal ball! Laughing aloud at that, she reached out and stroked Rosie who was stretching after a long snooze. As the cat ensconced herself on Sue's lap, her mobile rang and she was delighted to see it was her granddaughter. While Rosie padded on her thighs, she and Kate chatted for the next half hour and caught each other up with their news.

But although Sue would love to be able to fill in the blanks, Kate was not about to share her own discoveries. Not now. Not yet. Perhaps not ever.

CHAPTER TWENTY-SIX

1901 York

Kate had attended church the following Sunday, a late spring day in April, warm with the promise of summer days ahead, the blossom now bursting on the hawthorn trees that lined the walks in the park. As usual, they took the now regular walk together after the service, with James racing ahead and scattering the birds that were vociferous in their courtships, renewing the pattern for the coming year.

Herbert was on tenterhooks, having sneaked looks at Kate throughout the interminable sermon in the hope of getting a clue about her answer. Kate gave him no indication of what her answer might be, even though she had already known it from almost the first moment that he had made the proposition.

After finding a bench to sit on, Kate savoured the warmth of the sun on her shoulders but was careful to shield the pale skin of her face from its rays under her black hat, embellished with black net and some black crepe flowers she had stitched upon it. Herbert perched on the edge of his seat, his eyes apparently on young James, but in truth his mind on what Kate's response might be. They passed the next few minutes in some idle chatter, then Kate took pity on him and gave him her full attention.

"I should like to take you up on your proposal Mr Davis. My landlady is becoming extremely unpleasant, and I fear I shall not have a roof over my head for much longer. I have paid my rent for the last week of this month, but then an alternative will have to be found. Would that suit your plans?"

Herbert visibly exhaled, as if he had been holding his breath for minutes. A hint of a smile creased his lips as he nodded his head and assured her that it would indeed be quite suitable.

"Ah will be takin' over the house in a few days an' then ye are at liberty to move in any time after that, that suits 'ee. 'Ave tha much to bring?"

Kate assured him that her possessions were few – mainly her clothes in one trunk and a few other items which were quite easily transported. They arranged that Herbert would collect them with a hand barrow at the end of the week. The house came partially furnished, he said, using the term loosely, for there was a bed in the room she would occupy and a kitchen table and a couple of chairs and not much else. He would take his own possessions along over the next day or two.

By the beginning of the next week, Kate and Herbert were settling into a new routine. At first, Herbert's younger boy, Amos, was shy and was unsure about this new person in his life. James, however, was delighted to have her company every day and came racing back from school, rather than dragging his feet as he usually did. She soon realised that her dressmaking business would have to be scaled down somewhat, as taking over the household duties soon took up the larger part of her time. But in return she had security, company and most importantly, somewhere she could bring her own child into the world without fear of being on the streets without any support.

They settled into a routine over the next few months. Herbert had managed to bring a motley collection of furniture and household items from his previous address, and Kate tried to add some more homely touches in the way of soft furnishings – new curtains for the front room, some cushion covers, an antimacassar for Herbert's chair, covers for the worn pillows in her bedroom. It was plain and basic living without many of the fancy frills she had grown up with, but it was better than the alternative. You have to make your bed and lie on it, she mused on more than one occasion.

The weeks passed and the hot summer days began to take their toll on Kate as her belly grew and her energy flagged. Having kept to her story about being a recently widowed woman for the sake of the neighbours, she drew some sympathy from a few of them but a few frosty glances from others. Herbert met them with his head held high and felt no compunction about explaining their arrangements – all above board, he was able to assure them, and convenient for both of them – a housekeeper and someone to look after his lads, and a welcome bit of extra rent as well.

As August settled on the city bringing heavy days with no wind, the oppressive atmosphere left Kate feeling exhausted. Young Amos was very demanding, a lively two-year old, and she encouraged James to take him out for a walk after school to give her a break. Bending over the sink to soak a cloth with cool water to mop her brow, she felt the first pangs that had her gasp and grip her belly. Grasping the hard edge of the kitchen table, she lowered herself on to a chair until it passed. By the time Herbert arrived from work a few hours later, she had managed to summon the midwife who lived lower down the street and make it upstairs to lie on her narrow bed, wreathed in sweat.

Herbert kept the lads occupied out in the small back yard, not wanting to hear the sounds that made his blood run cold. As the sun sank below the horizon, turning the sky vibrant shades of pink and gold, a new life arrived in Lowther Street. Kate gave birth to a healthy baby girl.

CHAPTER TWENTY-SEVEN

2018 Lincoln

Sue opened the now-familiar brown envelope from the Record Office and smoothed out the folded certificate inside.

YORK	Where and When Born	Name, if any	Sex	Name and Surname of father	Name, Surname and maiden name of mother	Occupation of father	Signature, description and residence of informant	When Registered
	Fifth of August 1901	*Eliza Kate*	*F*		*Kate Eliza Hoxton*		*Kate E Hoxton, mother, Lowther St. York*	*Tenth of August 1901*

That explained where Kate had given birth to her daughter, but it didn't help with discovering who the father was. Two steps forward and one step back! So Kate had returned to York and was there in the month of the census in 1901 – and she was already pregnant by the look of the dates. And then here she was a few months later, giving birth to her daughter but no named father. What a mystery.

Looking back through her folder, she located the marriage certificate for Kate that she had sent for previously.

When married	Name and surname	Age	Condition	Rank or Profession	Residence at time of marriage	Father's name and Surname	Rank or profession of father
Eighteenth of October 1902	*Herbert John Davis*	*32*	*Widower*	*Labourer*	*Lowther St, York*	*Albert Henry Davis (dec)*	*Labourer*
	Kate Eliza Hoxton	*26*	*Single*	*Dressmaker*	*Lowther St, York*	*William Hoxton (dec)*	*Waterman*

Was this man Davis the father? And if so, why wait so long after her daughter's birth to marry? Was his wife still alive at the time Kate got pregnant? Or was it a completely different set of circumstances altogether?

*****

Kate felt that they were now a family. Her feelings towards Herbert, or Bert as he preferred, had softened as the months had passed. She had no doubt that he had always been attracted to her, but she could not pretend that she had felt the same, certainly not initially. But living in the same house and sharing family mealtimes in the kitchen and cosy evenings by the fireside had built up a sense of companionship that Kate had never felt, and slowly that grew into a loving relationship. When Bert eventually screwed up his courage to broach a more permanent and intimate arrangement, Kate accepted. After all, what were her options?

James had always enjoyed her company and loved having her as his new Ma, not feeling at all put out that she might usurp the place of his own mother, he only being four years old when she had died. As for Amos, he had never known anyone as his mother, the only carer being the landlady who used to watch him when Bert was working, and she was not about to lavish any affection upon him. Where James was boisterous and cheeky, even a little forward and outspoken, Amos was a quiet and intense child, often frowning and thinking carefully before making a statement or giving an opinion.

Kate and Herbert were married quietly at the Register Office and had a few of their acquaintances to a wedding breakfast at a local inn nearby. After that, their lives returned to the comfortable arrangement they had previously established, except this time they shared a bed and a closeness that Kate found both welcome yet unfamiliar. Of course, Bert expected that she would have been familiar with marital relations, having become pregnant by her sailor before he had died. Yet her shyness and nervousness he took for modesty and propriety, which he found both becoming and a stimulus to his ardour. As for Kate, she had no way to explain to him or herself about her lack of experience, but soon discovered that Bert was patient and gentle, so she could desire for nothing more.

Their life settled into a happy and comfortable routine. Once James was off to school, she fed the two younger children. Amos, now nearly four was content to play with his bricks and toy train upon the kitchen floor while she fed baby Eliza – or Lizzie as they all called her. Although she had named the baby after her beloved aunt Eliza, she felt happier giving her a name to herself. She was a cheeky little girl, spoiled by all the males in her life. Although not his own daughter, Bert adored her and Kate imagined that she was probably a replacement for the little one he had lost. Without thinking, he would refer to her as Lizzie Davis, unconsciously giving her his name as well as his affection. She had a most engaging gaze and would look so intently at her audience while trying to speak, frowning if she couldn't get their attention. Young Amos did not resent her, thankfully, and seemed pleased not to be the baby anymore and be the big brother instead.

In the summer of the following year, Kate felt a familiar clutch at her stomach as she counted the weeks and realised her courses were late. But this time, she could look forward with hope, not fear, with security, not trepidation.

*****

Kate awoke with a start, sweat drenching her bed. Throwing back her duvet, she gratefully felt the cooler air waft over her legs. Had she been in a dream? A nightmare? She felt confused at first and couldn't ground herself either in the past or the present. Her belly lay flat, her hip bones protruding slightly above her knickers. Her oversized tee shirt was bunched up under her and her hair had worked its way loose from the scrunchie used to keep it off her face during the night. The encumbrance of the linen nightdress was slipping from her memory but she turned, half expecting to see another form beside her in the half-light of morning. Laying her hand across her abdomen, the shock of feeling no tight swelling of overstretched skin made her gasp until the buzzing of her phone on the bedside table intruded upon the silence, announcing her morning alarm call which pulled her back to the present. With a jolt she realised what being pregnant must feel like. What was the significance of this link to the past? Kate realised by now that she was being 'summoned' when there was a time of extreme emotion – happy or sad.

But the insight was not complete. She had discovered no outcome. She needed to return. She needed to learn more. She lay, breathing deeply and willing herself to be lying in the narrow bed with Bert's shoulders against her back and the comforting rotundity of her belly keeping her company while he snored, blissfully unaware.

But all she heard was the door of Jen's bedroom slamming followed by the cascade of water in the shower. All she saw was the crack of light between the vertical blinds, pulled shut against the morning sun. All she felt was the sense of loss and emptiness akin to when a dear friend waves farewell.

CHAPTER TWENTY-EIGHT

1905 York

Kate looked down at the tiny infant in her arms. His crushed pink face creased and a wavering cry emanated from him as Bert leant over and looked down on his newly arrived son. It had not been an easy pregnancy, not like Lizzie's. Kate had been dizzy and nauseous for the last couple of weeks and suffered frequent headaches. At times she could hardly walk up the incline from the market, having to stop to catch her breath, and once she had momentarily blacked out on the doorstep when she had eventually made it home.

And then, too early, she had severe pains which she initially dismissed but soon realised were labour pains. The midwife had rushed to the house and from her face, Kate knew that she was concerned. Usually a garrulous woman, she was now a woman of few words, her mouth set in a grim line, her mind focussed on saving both, if possible, one if that was the way it must be. Kate was so weak that she thought she would never be able to deliver the babe, but when he eventually arrived, he was tiny, blue and lifeless. The midwife took him over to the other side of the room and rubbed him briskly with the towel that she had wrapped around him. After what seemed like a lifetime, the merest little whimper was heard and after a few more querulous cries, he slowly turned pink.

The midwife gently suggested that they might like to get him baptised soon, and from that Kate realised that she had concerns about his life expectancy. They named him Henry Charles and his birth date was Good Friday. He was very small and did not take to the breast as easily as Lizzie had. What little she could encourage him to swallow often came back up. When she laid him down, she took to watching over him as his tiny chest gasped for air, sometimes quivering as he fought for the next breath. She barely slept and kept him beside her on the bed, held close for warmth and comfort.

Bert took the children to Easter Sunday service alone and bade them hush when they returned, each with a chocolate egg he had bought for them. Easter Monday came but it was obvious to Kate that her darling boy was slipping from her, just like his namesake had slipped away all those years before. Cradling him in her arms, she saw the flutter of the little eyelids, so thin and transparent with their tracery of fine blue veins before his little chest gave up the fight for air and he slipped so sweetly into a sleep from which he would never awaken. She sat rocking him for an hour or more before she relinquished him to the care of the midwife, summoned by Bert when he had discovered his wife, her face pale and tear streaked. Unbeknownst to anyone, she had taken her tiny sewing scissors and snipped the merest wisp of his hair, not quite dark and not quite fair, not quite wavy but not quite straight. Before making the final snip, she tied a length of fine, pale blue silk from her workbox around them to keep the tiny strands together.

The funeral was simple. He was laid to rest in the cemetery on the southern outskirts of the city with Bert's first wife and his baby daughter. The simple stone would have his name added in due course and there he would remain, unknown and unremembered until someone in the future might search for a scrap of evidence to give him substance again.

*****

Kate's 'bouts of melancholy' returned. She slept badly and often awoke, laying her hand on her flat belly and crying out aloud with anguish at feeling its concave emptiness. Her cries woke Bert and he would hold her in his arms and rock her until she fell asleep, but more often he drifted off and she was left staring into the gloom, silent tears soaking her pillow. As spring gave way to summer, she would rise early when she had one of these episodes and dressing quickly, sit in the old wooden rocking chair in the cold kitchen, the embers of the stove barely holding any heat before being stirred to action for the morning breakfasts.

On one of these occasions, she could not settle and, although it was still very early, the sun was already above the horizon and finding its way into the gaps between the terraced houses. She threw a thin coat over her shoulders and walked down to the park where she could sit alone with her thoughts on the bench overlooking the river. How could her little one have been taken so soon, before she had even got to know him, before he had recognised his name, before he had learned to recognise her soothing voice and take nourishment from her breast?

I am always here.
You can come and visit me any time. We are one.
We are closer than you think.
I enjoyed your last visit.
That's a dance we can perform any time you feel lonely and need my company.
And what an outcome!
I'm sure we could have fun again.

The hairs on the back of Kate's neck crept and she shivered involuntarily, even though the warmth of the sun could already be felt upon her shoulders. What did 'it' mean? A hazy memory, shreds of gauzy images swimming just out of reach like the swirling eddies of grey water. The glint of light, steely upon the leaden surface, then dark depths that swallowed her up, but held her close like the embrace of a possessive lover. Then the curtains closed upon the scene and there was nothing.

Not content with invading her mind through her sleepless nights, now it stalked her waking hours and entered uninvited.

She clamped her hands over her ears in an attempt to silence it, but if anything, its words were even clearer without the hum of the waking city. The horses' hooves, the clatter of the market stalls being set up, the rumble of the barrow boys' carts on the cobbles, the distant chiming of a church clock, the chatter of ducks upon the quayside, the watermen's calls to greet each other before the next day's journeys scattered them, the swash of the river as it lapped on the staithes....

She started rocking in a frantic attempt to distract her from the invasion taking place in her mind, her eyes clamped shut and her fingers clenched in her hair, now falling loose from where she had hastily scraped up and secured it with a clasp.

"Kate, Kate!"

No, there it was again! It called her name, it knew her.

"Kate, Kate! I'm here!"

"No!" she shouted, thrashing out wildly at the hands that held her wrists and pulled her hands away from her face.

"It's me! It's Bert! Open yer eyes, 'ere look, tis me."

Not daring to open her eyes yet feeling a familiar embrace and hearing a voice that brought her comfort, she eventually calmed down and slumped on the seat, barely able to hold herself from sliding to the ground.

"Bert?" was all she could manage to croak before she collapsed into his arms. Thankfully there were not many passers-by in the park, the hour being still early.

"I found 'ee gone, an' nowhere in't house. Ah couldn't think where 'ee'd be but something made me look 'ere. Come away lass. Let me take 'ee back 'ome. Yer all right now. Ah'm 'ere."

Allowing him to wrap his jacket around her shoulders, she stood on shaking legs and allowed herself to be guided through the awakening streets. Once home, Bert took her up the stairs and made her lie down upon the bed, covering her with one of her homemade quilts, before heading downstairs to rake up the stove and feed the children. Assuring them that their mother just needed to rest, he shooed them out to school, before making sure that she was all right. He found her deeply asleep, for once, and rather than wake her he crept out and closed the front door silently before heading off to work, leaving her a note scrawled with a stub of a pencil on the back of an old brown paper bag, which he smoothed out and left upon the bedside table.

'Gone to work. Children fed. Have let you sleep. Hope you will be all right. Will be back at dinnertime. Rest well. Bert X'

And sleep she did. By the time he returned at midday for his dinner, she was breathing deeply and calmly for the first time in many weeks. As he was about to leave her, she stirred and stretched out under the coverlet, and seeing him silhouetted against the sunlight now entering through the thin curtains, she stretched out her hand to grasp his.

"Are 'ee all reet?" he whispered.

"I – I think so. How did I get back here? I can hardly remember. I feel like I have been asleep for weeks."

"Ye scared me, ah'll say that. Ye 'ad one of yer bad dreams but ye must 'ave left 'th'ouse. I found 'ee down at park by t'river. 'Ow are ye feelin' now?"

"I feel better than I have for a long while, Bert. I'm sorry I caused you such worry. Are the children all right?" she added, making to rise from the bed.

"They're fine. All at school. Ye can rest a bit more if ye 'ave a mind to?"

"No, no, I feel much improved. Let me up, Bert, and get you back to work. I'll see you later. Don't worry, please." And with that she put her arms around his neck and gave him a peck on his cheek to send him on his way.

As the front door closed, she stood by the window and watched him set off down the road. Taking a deep breath, she felt she had broken through a barrier she had been in danger of being crushed by. And she felt lighter, freer, more in control than she had for a long time.

Unbeknownst to her, Bert made a detour as he returned from work that afternoon and went to the Register Office to register both the birth and the death of their little son. He never told Kate, fearing she would not be able to think about this and dreading plunging her back into the abyss.

*****

Kate didn't fall pregnant again. Secretly she felt relieved and doubted whether she could face another loss, if that was to happen again. Perhaps her body knew that too. Bert was always hopeful that they might have another son, but it was not to be. Kate adored her Lizzie and made sure that she was beautifully dressed, making her little coats cut down from the ones the boys outgrew, embellished with frogging or buttons, velvet collars or a fur muff. She was the envy of her playmates, and soon Kate had a steady stream of mothers at her door bringing items for her to remake for their own little girls. Soon she added hats to her repertoire and was able to adorn them with scraps left over from her dressmaking orders, which she still did for the better-off ladies of the town.

Bert, having always been a labourer and a good reliable worker, found himself a new position with the Parks Department. It meant a steady wage and security. He would be digging new flower beds in the spring, laying out the summer planting, clearing up the leaves in autumn or shoring up saplings against the winter storms. He always loved being outside and often

James would meet him after school wherever his father was working, and they would walk home together. When he left school at fourteen, James joined the council as a labourer, doing the more manual work and in the process, he became strong and his shoulders broadened as he developed muscles and a broad frame as he grew into a strapping young man. Sometimes he would be working in the cemetery, digging graves and occasionally his father would be with the gardeners putting in summer bedding in the areas by the gateway.

With Bert's secure job and James' extra income, the family were able to move to a bigger property in Granby Road. It had its own little front garden, more of a patch pocket of earth, but Bert always had something growing there. It had a back yard, big enough to hold a couple of vegetable plots in raised beds and Bert trained a cordon apple along the sunny wall to the side. Another advantage was that Kate could use the larger parlour to leave her new sewing machine permanently in situ on its oak table. It had been Bert's treat to her as a moving-in present. He had come across it second-hand and got it at a knock-down price. James and Amos still shared a room. Lizzie had the little box-room which was set into the attic space and they had a small bathroom off the scullery downstairs. As the second decade of the twentieth century unrolled, they were happy and life seemed settled and secure. But the world was already changing and in a few short years their lives, and those of their neighbours and countrymen, would be changed forever.

*****

Sue opened up her folder and looked at the 1911 census she had previously downloaded and printed out for the family. There they were, living at 9 Granby Road in York. Herbert's two sons and Kate's daughter Eliza, recorded with the surname of her stepfather. Acknowledging he was the father perhaps? Or just adopting her as one of the family?

It was when Sue took a second look at the 1911 census that she realised that the columns for births read: *total children born* 2, *total children born alive* 1, *children who have died* 1. She needed to find the missing child. She turned to FreeBMD and looked for any children born in York with the surname Davis between 1903 and 1906. There were five. Then she looked for any deaths in that same period. Another half dozen. Finally she looked at both sets of names side by side and could confirm that only one had been born and died within that period, age at death being 0. And so she found him. Henry Charles Davis. And saying his name aloud meant he was not forgotten nor lost forever...

CHAPTER TWENTY-NINE

2018 York

Kate sat staring at the writing slope, looking incongruously antique against the slick lines of the Ikea flat-pack furniture in her room. She had been researching their history and references to them in literature through the ages, in preparation for the essay and presentation she would be giving after the Christmas break.

She had learned that the earliest writing slopes, desks or boxes, were made of solid hardwoods. The campaign box or desk was a necessary piece of equipment used by officers in the British Army and were most often made of solid mahogany throughout the Regency period. Later they might be made of a lesser hardwood like rosewood, with a more stylish veneer. They were made to lock so that the contents remained secure while on board steamers or trains, carriages or carts. Most importantly, the interior usually had various compartments to hold glass ink bottles, stamps, blotters, pens and other items. The folding writing surfaces were of tooled leather and lifted up to reveal storage beneath, as well as hidden drawers and secret compartments.

Many examples of great literature as well as dispatches, contracts, official documents, love letters and postcards from all parts of the Empire would have been written on them and there were recorded examples of their use by Jane Austen, Alexander Pope, Charles Dickens, Oliver Goldsmith and Lord Byron, to name but a few.

By now she was totally immersed in the study of the writing slope as an object that both featured in, and contributed to, the greatest literary works of history. She had no such delusions about her own scruffy example which sat opposite on the bedroom chest of drawers. Something drew her to go over to it and apologise for her harsh thoughts. 'You're not made of any fancy hardwood with intricate veneer or tooled leather, are you?' she mused. 'But still, you must have had a part to play in my history.' And once more she unfolded it and laid back the scruffy leather lid. She had returned the shell to sit within its compartment, as she felt that that was where it belonged, but curiosity made her locate the little hidden catch that would open it, so that she could feel it in her hand again.

The low sun was streaming into her room and almost blinding her. She was about to close the compartment again when something caught her eye, something she had never noticed before – a tiny blue fibre sitting deeper inside the cavity which had held the shell. Lifting and tilting the slope, she brought the sunlight to shine deeper into the tiny space. She could still not make out what might be in there, so she had to resort to flicking on the torch of her phone and aiming the beam directly into the compartment. There was definitely something in there but she couldn't make out what it was. Finding a pair of tweezers in her make-up bag lying on the dressing table, she gently poked them deeper into the gap and tweaked at the item until she could get a tenuous hold on it. Very slowly and carefully she drew it out and into the light of day. There lay the merest wisp of hair, not quite dark and not quite fair, not quite wavy but not quite straight, secured with a few strands of faded baby-blue silk thread. And strangely Kate was not surprised. There was a familiarity about it that she could not comprehend. But also a feeling of deep sadness and loss. Slowly she understood…

CHAPTER THIRTY

1914 York

The morning of the 29th July shone bright and clear, with a promise of the continued warmth of the last few days. But all the backyard fence and doorstep talk was of the news of the previous day – the declaration of war. Mothers' hearts were full of dread while the youths' were full of bravado. For the Davis family, the repercussions of this announcement had not been fully appreciated, but as the weeks wore on it became clear that the whole country was now worked up into a frenzy of patriotism and duty.

By the end of that year, it was obvious that the boast that the war would be over by Christmas was a hollow one. Bert's work continued much as before but James was getting itchy feet and, with so many of his friends joining up, he felt he should do the same. He was now nineteen and a strong young man, used to outdoor physical work. An ideal candidate for the army, so all his mates told him. The whole region was shocked when one December night, towns along the East coast, including Scarborough and Whitby, were shelled by German battleships.

The following day James and Bert left together for work but by the early evening, only Bert had returned. They usually met up somewhere along their familiar route home and walked the last few streets together. But tonight was different. As Bert passed the recruiting posters stuck on the fences and walls along his familiar homeward route, his stomach sank and he offered up a silent prayer. Another hour passed before the knob rattled and James came in the back door, stamping his feet to shake off the light snow that had fallen.

"Where've ye been lad? Yer mother's kept yer dinner warm for 'ee," Bert remonstrated with him.

After hanging his coat upon the hook behind the door, the lad looked down sheepishly at his feet before taking a deep breath and announcing to the family, still sitting round the kitchen table, "Ah've joined up."

His announcement was met with a heavy silence for a few moments as each one of them took in the information. First to speak was his younger brother, Amos. "Lucky sod! Wish ah wus old enough!"

"Dear God!" was Kate's response, as her hand clamped over her mouth to stifle any further words.

Lizzie just stared and then started to cry.

Bert stood, grabbed his work jacket off the back of his chair and announced he was off to the yard to dig up a cabbage for tomorrow's dinner. "But it's started to snow," James called after him, as if it made any difference. Bert couldn't find the words and he needed to get away before he said something he'd regret.

It was a miserable Christmas. Everyone was trying to show forced cheerfulness while at the back of their minds was the thought that James would be off on New Year's Eve to join the rest of the recruits before marching off to the barracks south of the city. In his meagre pack was a scarf knitted by his little sister, a thick pair of woolly gloves and two pairs of socks knitted by Kate, a tin of Rowntrees sweets from Amos and a box of tobacco and cigarette papers from Bert.

Along the streets, the groups of young men swelled in number, all heading off to join the 1/5th West Yorkshire Regiment, to beat the Hun, to win the War and come home heroes. As the rhythmic stamping of their marching feet disappeared into the distance, families held hope in their hearts that their boy would be coming home again soon, safe and well, but with dread in the pit of their stomachs that it might be last time they would ever feel their arms around them giving them a hug, with a cheery, "That's me off muther!" as they walked out through the door.

*****

Amos turned fifteen that spring and having left school, had been working at Border's, the grocer in Coney Street. With so many young men joining up, they were glad of a boy to deliver orders, mind the shop and sweep up at the end of the day. But Amos was a restless soul and hated having to follow orders and mooch about the shop, doling out flour, weighing out tea or fetching down tins to put in the housewives' baskets, while listening to them talk about what their husband or sons might be doing at the front. He used to walk back home, along the river, kicking at stones, hands stuffed deep into his pockets and chin buried in his collar. He'd been a poor scholar and often got into trouble for using his fists too hastily in response to an ill-considered word from one of the other youths, also just itching to leave the confines of school. A group of them would often hang about the staithes, watching the watermen load their barges, keen to lend a hand, but more often getting sworn at for getting in their way. His father would shake his head when he turned up with another black eye or scraped fist, usually extolling him to 'be more like yer brother' which only served to make him even more resentful of James.

James – always so cheery, everyone's friend, a magnet for the cheery smirks from the lasses on a Sunday after church. God, he'd be even more puffed up when he'd come home in uniform! Amos became evermore moody and sullen, never answering in words when a grunt would suffice. At home, he'd eat his meal in silence then retreat to the room he had to himself now that James had left. Occasionally his father would call him down to lend a hand with a job in the backyard, but more and more he spent the evening hours in his own company. When he could, he'd get hold of a newspaper from the previous day and cut out any pictures or articles about the war, making up a scrapbook in an old school notebook.

*****

James came home on leave in late March. The whole household was in uproar. Lizzie was screeching in delight at her handsome brother in his ill-fitting brown uniform and cap with its shiny regimental badge dead centre. Kate insisted that they get a portrait done at the photographers and Bert simply clapped the lad on the back, a man of few words as usual. From what James said, it was likely that the battalion would be mobilised soon, having completed their training which, he said with a wry smile, seemed to consist mainly of marching – fast, slow, in formation and for hours on end. And doing bayonet drill. Which impressed Amos a bit more.

The two days' leave flew by and before they knew it, James was off with his kitbag slung over his shoulder, shiny boots squeaking as he stomped off down the road, causing passers-by to wave and shout, 'good luck' and wish him well. The house seemed very quiet after he had left, and they settled back into their usual routine. Bert had the photograph of his son framed and set in pride of place in the parlour on the mantelpiece.

A few weeks later James was able to send a postcard home from France with a few scribbled words assuring them all was well. But soon his division would be joining up with many others to become the force fighting on the Western Front. By the second week in May, James and his comrades had their first experience of sitting in the trenches in the rain and coming under fire. And seeing men die and be stretchered away wounded and crying out for their mothers. It was to be known as The Battle of Aubers Ridge.

From his room in York, his brother was eagerly scanning the newspaper reports days, weeks later as news of the battalion's exploits were reported. These, he eagerly cut out and added to the growing scrapbook.

*****

The years dragged on. The War dragged on. And at about the same time as James was ducking as shells exploded near his dugout in Northern France, a Zeppelin attack in early May 1916 dropped eighteen bombs on the city of York and killed nine people and injured forty more. The citizens of York were even more conscientious in ensuring their curtains were drawn tightly across and lights extinguished before opening their doors. Conscription was introduced that year, but Kate was thankful that Bert was above the age of those able-bodied men required to join up. Servicemen thronged the town as so many were stationed in and near the city. Schools had to house servicemen and a tented village was set up at Knavesmire, near the racecourse, south of the city. The women of the town took over many of the jobs that the men had done – tram drivers, ambulance drivers or factory workers, and earned the same as the men in many instances.

Every so often the Lord Mayor would puff out his chest, his chain of office glinting in the sunlight, as he extolled the virtue of fighting for one's country from the steps of the recruiting office, which was in Exhibition Square. And then he returned to his well-appointed home and put up his feet while he read the latest newspapers, having roused the next group of York's young men to join up and lay down their lives in some far-off foreign field.

James had two more lots of leave, each time returning home as a shadow of the man he had been previously. His eyes were dark and sunken, his face grey and his soul broken by what he had seen and those he had lost alongside him. But he did come home. He was one of the lucky ones. He'd had a dose of trench foot and been treated for it. The little finger on his left hand had been hit by a piece of shrapnel from a shell burst that cut through the man next to him, but mercifully left him virtually unharmed. At least physically.

As the war limped on through 1917, and the nation hoped for peace, Amos, now eighteen, pasted the last article into his scrapbook, now running to three volumes, and signed his name at the bottom of his enlistment papers. No longer would he sit and read the exploits of others. It was time for him to get out there and make a difference. No more sweeping up and delivering groceries. No more sly looks from the girls, wondering why he wasn't doing his bit. No – now he would show them!

CHAPTER THIRTY-ONE

2018 Lincoln

Sue packed up the notes she had made into her ever-growing folder. This evening at the family history class the tutor had focussed on Service Records and what could be found in them. Sue had scribbled some references down and collected the handouts about where various records might be located, both online and in person. As she didn't even know if her family tree had any service personnel upon it, she didn't feel much connection to the examples the tutor had flashed up for them to study. However, the tutor did say that any research around family living in the first half of the twentieth century was pretty sure to throw up some men who had either joined up or been casualties.

When she sat down at the kitchen table next morning, she looked back at the census information she had for the Davis family. Flipping open her folder at the one for 1911, the closest one to the First World War, she could see that Kate's stepsons, James and Amos, were sixteen and twelve years old respectively. So from the years 1914-1918 James would be aged nineteen to twenty-three, and Amos would be fifteen to nineteen. So there was a fair chance that one, maybe even both would have some kind of service recorded. And what about their father? Herbert was forty-one years old on the 1911 census and, if she remembered correctly what the tutor had said, conscription was only for men up to forty-one years of age; Herbert would be too old by the time war broke out.

Looking again at the tutor's notes, she realised that she needed to log on to FindMyPast to view and download Service Records so decided that she would head off to the public library after lunch. Next, she searched for the Commonwealth War Graves site, in case either of the boys had been killed and commemorated on some far-off foreign field. Looking for James Davis, she found there were 32 British soldiers of that name but there was no record for Amos Davis, although four records with the surname Davies. Until she could find out more from the military records on FindMyPast, she would be on a bit of a wild goose chase. She decided that when she was in the library, she would also have a look at some of the Archive Newspapers online and find out any information about York in the war years, to give her a bit of background. Folding up her notes, she packed them into her well-used 'bag for life' and snapped on the radio to listen to the news while she made a cup of tea and checked the mail that had just flopped through the letterbox.

Rosie followed her into the kitchen, rubbing herself against Sue's legs and meowing pitifully. "You'd think you were never fed, my lovely!" Sue exclaimed, but nevertheless, sprinkled a few cat treats on the mat, which Rosie soon hoovered up gratefully before stalking off to sit on the windowsill and keep an eye on the bird table.

*****

By the time Sue arrived home, it was already growing cold and dark. There was a suggestion of frost in the air and the sky was deep black with a sprinkling of stars and a crescent moon just visible through the trees opposite her cottage. Pulling her hand-knitted scarf tighter around her neck, she slid the key in the lock and gratefully felt the warmth hit her as she staggered into the hallway, the overloaded bag threatening to slide off her shoulder before she could shut the door behind her. Rosie greeted her with the familiar demand for food, but first she shed her layers of clothing and switched on the kettle, needing a warm drink to thaw her out. By the time they were both fed – a hastily heated up cottage pie in the microwave for Sue and a chicken liver and trout sachet for Rosie, she was ready to tackle organising the information she had found into some semblance of order.

Initially she had been disappointed to find that, having trawled through all the James Davises, the record she eventually located was simply an enlistment form and a rather sparsely filled-in sheet with initials and dates purporting to refer to his war service. She would take them along next week to the class and try and make more sense of them with the tutor's help. A second trawl through the records for Amos, however, produced far more surprising results. She ended up with over twenty printed-out sheets about his war service, and from what she could see, it was not about his heroic exploits, rather they listed far less-flattering entries about punishments and fines. She needed time to sift through it all, get it into chronological order and try to find out what on earth had happened to Amos.

CHAPTER THIRTY-TWO

1917-1918 York

Lizzie had left school and joined many of the young girls of York, working at the Rowntrees factory. They felt they were doing their bit for the war effort, especially as there were so few young men in the town now. Not that there weren't loads of soldiers. Many were billeted in makeshift accommodation in schools and other available buildings, as well as in the various encampments beyond the city walls. And there were plenty of wolf whistles flying as the girls walked home from work, arm in arm, drawing the attention of the young men on leave in the town or just en-route to somewhere else. Trains huffed and puffed day and night, in and out of the station. Everywhere seemed to be on the move. Then, when each detachment left, there would be a few days of eerie quiet when the town would draw breath and heave a sigh, before the next onslaught of boisterous young men, flag waving and the sound of marching boots.

Lizzie was now so very like her mother in looks. The same hair, worn in a thick plait, the porcelain skin and slim figure. And her eyes – clear, almost bottomless, with a dark-lined iris that caught your attention and drew you in. And Lizzie knew it. She was aware of the heads that turned and the second glances but not yet skilled at flirting, she would often blush when a cheeky comment came her way.

Every morning she would set off along the street, linking up with other lasses headed for the factory. If the weather was inclement, they would crowd on the tram that took them the short distance to the north-east of the city, but mostly they would link arms and in groups of twos and threes, walk the distance to the Rowntrees factory, just over half a mile. On the way they would chatter about what news there was from their brothers or sweethearts, but sometimes they were needed to console one of their number who had received bad news from the front.

On arrival at the factory, they would don white linen pinafores and ensure their hair was well pinned back. Lizzie and her friend Edith were usually to be found sat next to each other on the long table where they packed fruit pastilles into boxes. Lizzie enjoyed the freedom from school, where, in her last year, she had been a student teacher. This really only meant working with the youngest children and helping them with their reading, writing and simple arithmetic. But it wasn't for her and she was itching to be able to earn a wage and be more independent.

On Sundays she would join Bert and Kate as they attended the local church a few streets from where they lived. She always felt proud of how smart she looked, thanks to her mother's dressmaking skills, and often drew admiring glances from her friends.

The house seemed very quiet now that both boys were at war. Bert withdrew into himself, fearing for the lads. He would take himself out into the back yard and spend hours bent over his vegetable plot or in his potting shed which he'd tucked into the gap between the back door of the house and the garden wall. Every day at work the men would talk about the latest news from the front, sharing newspapers to read over their lunch break. Sometimes one of them might have received a letter and they would crowd round the recipient while he painstakingly read it out to the assembled men. But sometimes one of their number would not turn up for work and the bad news would trickle through the group of a son who would not return, or if he did, would not be the man that had once departed so full of life and purpose. And each one of them would offer up a silent prayer of thanks that the news was not about their son – this time.

*****

When Amos left the shores of England, having had a few weeks of basic training, he found himself upon a heaving boat crammed with other men in similar uniforms that disgorged its human cargo at Boulogne. Loaded onto trains, they headed south to Étaples. In a couple of days he found himself and a few other men transferred to the Labour Corps. The thought that he would not have his chance in the front line left him crestfallen. After all, that was why he had joined up. He soon discovered that the Labour Corps units were often deployed for work within range of the enemy guns, sometimes for lengthy periods. Their job was to cook, clean, carry and care for the soldiers on the front line and behind the lines. They built roads and railways, carried the wounded and buried the dead. Throughout that year and the next, that was to be his war. And he saw plenty of things that would live with him for the rest of his life, and which he never wrote of in his letters home.

On Armistice Day, the eleventh of November 1918, York Minster was crammed with a congregation of 10,000 who attended the Service of Thanksgiving. Although it was a Monday, the workers of the city were given a day's holiday and streets were draped with flags and bunting as everyone celebrated and counted the days until their menfolk would come home. Lizzie and her friends dressed in their Sunday best and tied red, white and blue ribbons in their hair as they danced and cheered outside the Guild Hall. Soon her brothers would be home. Soon life would be back to normal.

But it was months before the men started trickling home. James was demobilised in early spring of 1919 and couldn't wait to get home. As the train pulled into York station, he had the door open and his feet on the platform before the train had come to a halt. And it wasn't just his family he wanted to see. He had a sweetheart in York. They'd met on his last leave and had written since then. He couldn't wait to pop the question, if Ethel would have him, but he knew he'd have to go home first.

A few men were being helped from the train, some on crutches, some with bandages round heads or hands. James was thankful he was physically untouched, barring the permanently bent little finger on his left hand. Throwing his kitbag over his shoulder he joined the throng of men heading for the exit, mingling with women and children who had heard that their men were due today. James hadn't known till last night that he'd be homeward bound today, so he decided to surprise his family. It was nearly midday so he hoped he'd catch his father home for his meal or Kate at work on her dressmaking. Stretching his legs to stride through the familiar streets towards home, he wasn't sure what the future would hold. Would he get his old job back? Or get another? If so, what?

He stood outside the familiar door, hesitating. Should he knock or should he go round the back? In the end, he walked round to the back gate and let himself into the yard. Some winter greens were still growing in the beds and a few carrot tops flopped, due to be picked imminently. There was a wash hung upon the line, the snow-white linens flapping in the cold spring breeze. A mop and bucket stood by the back door and a scrubbing brush and upturned pail sat on the back step. All such mundane objects, but a small thrill of familiarity warmed his heart. Pausing for just a moment, he turned the knob and let himself into the warm kitchen, smelling of fresh baked bread and a stew on the stove. Kate was at the sink, hands deep in the soapy water as she rinsed through some dishes. She turned and for a moment couldn't make out who was there but then let out a whoop and flung her soapy arms around his neck.

No words were needed. Her tight grip on him said it all. As the harsh woollen cloth of his jacket scratched her cheek, she could smell the tang of stale tobacco and sweat ingrained into it. James could detect a few stray threads of grey among her dark hair but otherwise, she was just the same and he gave thanks every day for her love and generosity in taking him and his brother on and caring for them as if they were her own.

Not long after, his father came through the door, momentarily stunned to see him sitting at the kitchen table, a mug of tea in his hands and a broad smile upon his face. Scraping back his chair, James stood and in a moment his father had his arms around him in an unaccustomed show of emotion. A man of few words, all he could say was, "Aye, reet good t'see thee lad," as he patted his son's back a couple of times, then stood back and took off his battered flat cap and collapsed into his usual chair. Lizzie was at work but word had spread through the town that a lot of the men were back and she flew down the street, hoping that James or Amos might be among them. Her squeals of delight as she discovered James in the kitchen, washed and shaved and in civvies by now, echoed round the house and no doubt this scene was repeated in a few score more homes that day in York.

CHAPTER THIRTY-THREE

Northern France June 1919

But as yet, there was no news of when Amos might come home. Indeed, he was still in northern France but word from England seemed to be that the demobilised men were returning to no prospect of employment and little in the way of hope for the future. He had no trade and no qualifications to do anything rather than labouring, and he was not about to return to the drudgery and monotony of his previous life. Army life wasn't that much better, but at least you got paid, fed and had some daily routine to follow.

And then the news of the Spanish Flu reached the men still abroad. The troops returning had brought it with them, infecting the civilians back home. 'Better off here' was the general opinion for those men who had no wives or sweethearts waiting for them. The weeks and months crept on and Amos, like many of his fellow soldiers, found themselves increasingly bored with the stagnant state of affairs and sought comfort and companionship in the small towns nearby. It passed the time and assuaged an urge.

With a group of his mates, he made the decision to re-enlist, sending a letter home and assuring his father that at least he'd be able to send regular money home and not find himself unemployed. The rough camaraderie of the army had become his succour.

For the next few months his group were assigned special duties. If he thought he was a tough man, given to few emotions, he learned otherwise. They were camped at Ronssoy in northern France, in the area which was to become synonymous with all the horror that war created – the Somme. Although it was now mid-summer, the battlefields still were mired in glutinous mud. The edges were drying and becoming caked hard, but much surface water lay about, fed by the unseasonably heavy rain that had fallen.

Having been either marched or transported to the blasted remains of a battlefield where neither tree nor building remained, with crater-pocked mud stretching into the distance, each of the soldiers in his squad of thirty-two men was supplied with two pairs of rubber gloves, two shovels, wooden stakes, canvas and rope, stretchers, wire cutters and a poisonous chemical called cresol. At first, he was mystified by what this collection of items would be needed for, but one of the older, more experienced chaps quickly put him and the other lads in the picture. A few faces turned grey and a couple of men were seen to cross themselves.

Their sergeant came up and barked out their orders. Divide up into pairs and set out across the barren field. Shout if anyone spots unexploded munitions (although they had been told that the area had been cleared). Look for any rifles or stakes protruding from the ground, perhaps bearing helmets or other items of military equipment. Alternatively there might be signs of partial remains or equipment strewn on the surface or protruding from the soil. Look out for evidence of rat holes – where the creatures had disturbed remains and small bones or equipment might have been brought to the surface. Finally, any areas of grass (precious little of that remaining, Amos thought) might be more vivid in colour due to buried remains, and any area of lying water that held remains might appear a greenish-black or grey in colour.

By now, realisation of their task had finally sunk in. The men were doubled up in pairs, in general an older man with a younger one. Amos was paired up with a Lancashire chap, Charlie Wilkinson, and together they set off cautiously across the field.

Each pair fanned out across the barren, blasted wasteland, heads down, eyes scanning the small patch of ground a few feet ahead and to the side, expressions grim and voices stilled.

At first, Amos thought they would find nothing, their route throwing up no sign, living or dead. Then, as they crested a small rise and looked down into the water-logged ditch at the further side, a flash of something light-coloured caught his eye. He glanced at Charlie, who had also spotted it, and together they slithered down the incline towards it. As they got closer it became clear that this was not stone, but bone. Shards of what looked like an arm or leg. The sergeant had made it clear what their next task should be upon locating any indication of remains. Donning their gloves, they both started to scoop away the mud around the bones, uncovering what looked like scraps of sodden material. A brass button glinted as it caught the light, half buried in the sludge. Their task now consisted of examining what remained for any identification such as regimental badges, indications of rank, anything metallic such as identity discs, clips on braces, belt buckles, etc. And then any pockets or wallets which might contain personal effects. Anything which might identify the individual.

Amos shuddered as his hands sank into the soft flesh which had turned to slime, searching for anything solid. The bile rose in his throat as he pushed aside a lump which might have been a limb and a mass of maggots writhed, having been uncovered at their gruesome task. It crossed Amos' mind that they were no better, sieving through the mass of decaying flesh for anything of worth. After about ten minutes of working through the remains, they had amassed a pathetic pile of personal items that might lead to a possible identification of the man who had once bravely faced the enemy and followed the orders that brought him to this ignominious resting place. A metal cigarette case. A waterlogged wallet which contained some family photos. A spoon. A few buttons. A crucifix on a leather thong. A few coins.

A lucky horseshoe charm.

Their next task was to place a stake at the site of their discovery. Amos held it while Charlie used the back of the spade to thump it into the soft soil. Stretching up to straighten his bent back, Amos took a moment to look around and saw others bent to the same task as themselves. Some were knee-deep in mud. Others were already moving from one discovery on to the next. Two men were on their knees with wire cutters, trying to free their discovery from a tangle of barbed wire which had claimed him. One young lad was bent double, throwing up his last meal. It was like a scene out of hell.

Having amassed all that remained of the man, they lay the remains on to the canvas which they had soaked in cresol, and then wrapped it around, tying it with rope. Nothing more than a numbered cross or circle drawn on a creased map would indicate the location. Later they would stretcher it back to be collected and labelled, along with the personal items which might serve to identify the man and eventually, give him a name that would be carved at his head upon a stone standing with thousands of others in a cemetery far from his native home.

*****

The force of the rifle butt hitting him in the small of his back caused him to be thrown onto the hard gravel. Two pairs of arms grabbed him and forced his hands behind his back, before shackling them. Frog marching him down the alleyway, they shoved him onto the back of a truck and pulled a tarpaulin over the back, shutting out any of the dim light that might have shown the other two faces of the occupants already in there. All he managed to see was the flash of a red cap before his knees crashed to the floor of the vehicle. He had been absent from camp for the last three days, before surrendering himself to the military police in Calais. Why had he headed north? Just the thought on that bright August day that he might be a few miles nearer home, a few miles away from the nightmare. Even now he couldn't recall how he made it that far. Feeling that all his waking and sleeping hours were crowded with the same images, he felt he had to break away. He felt his mental strength was draining from him and that he could not bear another day living in hell. But eventually, reality hit and he knew the chances of getting across the Channel without being apprehended were probably close to nil. And then, tired and hungry, the sight of the two redcaps patrolling the docks brought his situation into focus. It was well-nigh hopeless.

Brought up before his commanding officer the following day, he was charged with being absent from camp for three days and given field punishment and fined three days' pay. What went in his favour was the fact that he surrendered himself, rather than trying to evade capture.

*****

The summer days gave way to autumn, and his company continued with their grim task, each day a facsimile of the previous one, each bundle they wrapped and processed, just another nameless heap that had once been a man of flesh and blood, bone and sinew, hopes and fears and living for the joyous reunion with his loved ones upon his victorious return. Except that now no-one knew his whereabouts. No-one could lay flowers on his grave. No-one would touch his cheek and place a kiss upon his brow.

But the men undertaking this horrendous task were giving the fallen back their identities. That was the only way Amos could reconcile himself to the awful task he undertook day after unbearable day. The only relief was when they were allowed into the local town where they could find some kind of physical release with the opposite sex. Although officially frowned upon, it was generally accepted that the men needed to have the opportunity to 'enjoy' female company. The French had set up places to enable this very thing and they were run by older women who managed their girls accordingly. And although men were advised to take precautions, there was an advantage to disobeying this directive.

Sure enough, Amos contracted 'the clap', as it was generally referred to, and was relieved when his condition demanded treatment and he was shipped back home, finding himself at Cherry Hinton Hospital in Cambridge for three weeks over that Christmas. However, he didn't get in touch with his family. Perhaps he felt ashamed. Or perhaps he knew he wouldn't be able to try to answer their questions about what he had been doing in France. Instead he sent a card with the minimal in the way of best wishes for the season and assuring them he was well and hoping they were likewise.

*****

He still had many months of his enlistment to complete and found himself back in France, undertaking the same duties. Whenever he could, he and his mates would go off to the town and take some solace in the cheap wine and cheap women. Anything to dull the images that were the daily accompaniment to their lives. And his army record began to be peppered with a variety of misdemeanours. Eventually, as his term of enlistment came to an end, he was discharged as his services were no longer required due to his medical condition.

At long last he could return home. But the boy who had left was returning as a man who had seen too much and carried the torment of his nightmares buried deep in his inner soul.

CHAPTER THIRTY-FOUR

Lincoln 2018

Sue puzzled over the various abbreviations and illegible entries on the military record for Amos Davis. Having arranged the copied sheets into some semblance of chronological order, she was beginning to appreciate that Amos' military record was not filled with glory, but rather a sad and worrying catalogue of misdemeanours and punishments.

At the next family history evening class, the man next to her offered his help and together they started to unravel what had happened to Amos. Luckily Harry (that was his name) had had some experience of this from searching for military figures within his own family tree and had got to grips with some of the terminology. Bit by bit they started to work out what some of the acronyms and abbreviations meant and tied them in to the various dates noted.

What began as a very ordinary statement of military postings became an ever-more worrying litany of misdemeanours and detentions, fines and punishments. The lad who enlisted with his particulars noted as: *Height 5'6", weight 105lb, girth 32", expansion 2", dark complexion, grey eyes, brown hair,* underwent some sort of trauma that must have totally changed his character from *'very good'* to finally *'having been discharged with ignominy'*. It was heart-breaking to read.

Among the list of his misdeeds were: *Drunk at roll call – admonished. Drunk on return to camp – fourteen days punishment, fined 2/6, forfeit one day's pay. Missing from roll call at 20.00 hours – punishment 96 hours detention and fined 10/=. Using abusive language to Sergeant Crosby, awarded fourteen days' detention by*

Commanding Officer for misconduct. Relapse of disability due to carelessness in personal life.

At first, Sue wondered what 'disability' meant, assuming it was what someone in this century would imagine – damage to a limb, loss of sight, hearing, etc. but Harry cleared his throat, somewhat embarrassed, when he pointed to a coded entry and whispered, 'He had gonorrhoea'. Sue was momentarily taken aback, but Harry said that he had come across that entry on a few of his military ancestors' records, and that especially those who served in the First world War often returned home having been similarly infected. Life was brutal out there and they sought comfort where they could. Some even deliberately tried to catch it, so as to be removed from the front and receive treatment in a field hospital, or even returned to Blighty until they had recovered sufficiently to return to their duties. And the treatment was far from pleasant, Harry added with a shiver. Sue didn't press him further.

As they perused the documents further, and scanned down the Regimental Conduct Sheet, they found a section with an underlined heading: *Statement by soldier concerning his own case.*

The class looked up at Sue's sharp intake of breath as she clapped her hand over her mouth.

"Oh my God," she breathed. Harry merely nodded.

The words jumped out and seemed to explain it all now...

Statement by soldier concerning his own case:

What countries have you served?
    1918 - 1920 France

In what capacity?
    Exhumation of bodies

CHAPTER THIRTY-FIVE

York January 1920

By the time Amos arrived back in York, his kit bag slung over his shoulder, most of the men who were able to, had returned, and the list of those lost was being updated as word came from the Army when any remains were finally identified. If Amos took a small measure of pride in his role in that, the feeling of not fitting in to civilian life far overshadowed it. He never told the family what his precise duties had been. People talked about the war cemeteries that were being set up and relatives of the fallen were sent forms to complete which asked them their wishes as to the words to go on the memorial for their loved one. There was a huge disappointment that the bodies would not be repatriated but knowing what he had seen, Amos could understand why that would have been logistically far too great a task to undertake.

His father was overjoyed when his youngest lad walked through the door but, as always, showed the minimum of emotion. A handshake and a clap on the shoulder with a 'Reet good t'see thee lad,' welcomed him. Kate and Lizzie were more effusive and he welcomed the hugs and kisses from the women. And Lizzie was now certainly a young woman, not the girl he'd left behind. At seventeen, she had grown fuller in parts and slimmer in others, causing him to cast an appreciative eye over her before reminding himself that she was his little sister. She had changed her hairstyle to the more fashionable bob that all her girlfriends were now sporting. As well as being in vogue, it was also more practical for her job at the Rowntrees factory and much easier to cover in the cap or net required. Kate still hung on to her long hair, at Bert's bidding.

And now he had to think of getting a job. After days of trying to find one, he ended up labouring, taking work on a day-to-day basis as it came up. He ended up digging ditches at one of the outlying farms. Meanwhile James had returned to work back with his father in the parks department and much of his work at this time of year was tidying up the cemetery and, when required, digging graves. The irony of it wasn't lost on Amos. He had been digging them up and now his brother was burying them.

*****

It felt strange having the house full again. But it wouldn't be for long as James and his sweetheart, Ethel, were due to marry in the spring and already were saving up for the deposit on two little upstairs rooms and a kitchen at one of the terraced houses in the old part of the town. Kate and Ethel had hit it off immediately. Ethel also worked at Rowntrees, like Lizzie, and was a petite little blonde-haired lass with a ready smile and a ferocious temper, when roused. James would have his work cut out with her, mused Kate, but the lass loved the bones of him and they made a great couple, each complementing the other's nature. James gave in to her all the time, always laughing and gently berating her for her hasty words, but they were obviously meant for each other. Lizzie was beside herself with excitement at being a bridesmaid and of course, Kate was busily employed with making the dresses, veils and accessories.

Amos found settling back at home a challenge. Being surrounded by the daily routine felt superficial and he became increasingly restless. He slept only fitfully and though he wouldn't admit it to anyone, his dreams were pervaded by the images he had left behind on that foreign field. He made little effort to try to find employment although Bert occasionally mentioned possibilities he had heard about from his workmates. Amos would later respond with 'the job had already been filled' or 'they wanted someone with more experience' or 'they wanted someone older' – anything that would brush aside his father's enquiries. He met up with a couple of local lads who'd been with him in the battalion and they spent most of their time in one of the local pubs.

One evening, when James was out with Ethel and Lizzie had gone to choir practice, Kate and Bert sat together in the kitchen while Kate worked on hemming the skirt of what would be Ethel's wedding gown.

"Ah don't think that lad's ever goin' t'get a job," mused Bert. He looked shamefaced and suddenly, as if she had never noticed it before, Kate was acutely aware of the droop of his shoulders and the look of resignation in his eyes.

"Something'll turn up for him, don't you think?" mused Kate. A silence fell between them and Kate realised that in the weeks that had passed since the lad had returned, they had not had an opportunity to really have a proper conversation with Amos. Thinking about it more, Kate could visualise the haunted look in his eyes at times, the way he avoided talking about anything of his time in the army, the times he came down to breakfast looking like he hadn't slept. Those mornings Kate felt a shiver creep over her but didn't really register its presence.

CHAPTER THIRTY-SIX

York Summer 1920

Kate sat at the kitchen table, the bright summer sun flooding the room. The door was wide open and a gentle warm breeze stirred the flowers along the border of the path in the yard outside. The house was quiet and she had a pile of fabric spread out in front of her as she prepared to cut out the pattern for a blouse for Lizzie. Bert was at work. James, now a married man, was also at work and Amos – well Amos was out, doing whatever he did to fill his days. Kate sat back and leant against the hard wooden kitchen chair. She ran the back of her hand across her brow and felt the moistness brought on by the warmth of the day. A few pins were clamped tightly between her lips and a tape measure hung around her neck. It was only going to get warmer, the temperature already climbing although it was only mid-morning.

Pushing the fabric away from her, she stuck the pins into a pincushion and filled a glass with water from the tap at the Belfast sink. She could spare a few minutes, she assured herself, and walked out into into the bright sunshine. Bert had made a rough wooden bench which sat along the wall under the kitchen window, and she sank down gratefully upon it and closed her eyes, revelling in the warmth of the sun. The brightness still permeated her eyelids but she leant back, her head against the warm red bricks of the wall and allowed herself to breathe in the scents of the garden – the warm earth, the tang of the rosemary bush by the path, the heady perfume of the honeysuckle that she had trained up a wire over the door. A bee buzzed past her ear and she momentarily was startled but smiled to herself as it buried itself into the sweet flower in search of nectar.

Her thoughts strayed to her life as it was now, and what had gone before. She was content. She had security and a loving family. She shivered momentarily when she thought back to the days when she had first come to York, looking for work and then thrown out of her lodgings when she found herself pregnant. Life had a way of turning itself around. Now her days had moulded themselves into a comfortable routine.

Bert was a gentle, loving and considerate man. Not perhaps the most effusive or passionate of men, but solid, reliable and caring. What more could she wish for? Lizzie was just like her at that age. Dreaming of what her future might be, imagining herself swept off her feet like the heroine in one of the stories she read. But she was more excitable and vivacious than Kate had been at her age and would soon have them all laughing when she would prance around, mimicking one of the acts that visited the music halls.

James, although not her son, was just the child she would have wished for, had her little boy survived. Not a day passed that she didn't think of baby Henry and what he might have been like. He would have been seventeen now. But here was James, now a married man – and if Kate's intuition was correct, he would be a father before next spring. Ethel looked decidedly peaky when Kate had dropped by yesterday morning but the lass had said nothing and Kate didn't wish to pry. They would make a lovely little family, Kate mused. And she supposed that she would then soon be a grandmother, although in name only rather than by blood. She allowed herself to pull a wry face. Fancy that – her a granny – how old that made her feel!

And then there was Amos. Her face fell and a frown creased her brow. How did one describe Amos? A closed book perhaps. Hidden depths. Inscrutable. There always seemed to be a cool air around him, as if he was surrounded by an icy cloak. Laughter would stop when he entered a room. Conversations with him would be stilted and mainly monosyllabic. He carried a darkness with him that he never shared and into which he retreated. Kate was increasingly becoming uneasy when he was around but she could not say why exactly.

It was then she realised there was not a picture of Amos. On the mantlepiece in the front room was a photograph of her and Bert on their fifteenth wedding anniversary. It seemed like an extravagance but Bert had insisted. Beside it was a group photo of her and Bert with Lizzie taken on Lizzie's eighteenth birthday. Next to it was one in a dark wooden frame of James in his uniform on the eve of him being posted. Besides that, in a newer frame was the family wedding group taken just a few months ago. She sat back and tried to visualise it now, sitting in the peaceful garden. She could see the group now – all assembled in their finery. The older men looked uncomfortable in their stiff collars while the women had fussed about until they were sure their newly bought finery and accessories were shown off to their best advantage. James and Ethel stood side by side, almost afraid to smile but in the end, she recalled James had said something under his breath and Ethel had to suppress a giggle. Lizzie standing beside her as bridesmaid had not managed so well and was just about to burst out laughing when the photographer caught the moment. But Amos – Kate had to think hard to recall where he had been standing. Eventually, with a sigh, she stood and went into the house, walking through to the parlour to settle the question in her mind.

Stretching up, she took down the picture, vowing to do some dusting later, and scanned the faces. The relative gloom of the front room compared to the bright kitchen proved too much of an effort so she took it back through and sat down at the table propping it in front of her. As she scanned the group, her eyes jumping along the row of hats sported for the formal occasion, she eventually spotted Amos in the back row, half hidden behind a cousin of Ethel's. He was not even looking ahead but seemed to have his eyes focussed on something beyond the photographer. And with a start, she realised that yes, that was the only photograph of him that they had. She wondered if she might persuade Amos to go and get one done so that he would not feel overlooked on the mantlepiece assembly. She would ask him later, she decided, although she wasn't sure he would be very open to the suggestion.

*****

Amos walked slowly and deliberately up the dusty road, leaving the crowded streets of the town behind and cutting along the residential streets that led to home. Home. If you could call it that. A place to lay his head. He was getting sickened by that look of expectation from his father, the one that would greet him securing some job or other. But it wasn't going to happen, especially if he didn't even bother reading the adverts and notices. Plenty of returning men looking for jobs, happy to take anything to put money in their pockets. Well, not him. He had enough friends that he could meet and cadge a drink or two of, stretching it out to last the day before he had to show his face again. Sometimes he would have to resort to a bit of casual work – delivering some packages, digging a few ditches, something menial and pointless – that would give him some coins in his pocket to stand his round and ensure he got a few more in return.

The evening was hot and his throat felt dry and dusty. But his pockets were empty and his head already felt pleasantly fuzzy. Enough to start dulling his thoughts. He went in through the front door, correctly guessing that his father would be out in the back yard at his gardening, Kate probably sitting sewing on the bench beside him, chattering away about inconsequential events and hopefully, Lizzie would be either reading in her room or doing the dishes for her mother. His entrance was made in a few well-practised silent moves. His foot was on the stair and he was heading up before anyone had even heard the door click shut. As he reached the landing, he could hear Lizzie's voice in the kitchen below so he knew he was successful in his subterfuge. He wasn't in the mood for talking – was he ever – and all he wanted to do was stretch out, shut his eyes and blot out the recurrent images with deep, drink-sodden sleep.

Throwing his thin jacket over the chair, he lay back on the cool pillow and put his arms behind his head. Was this how it was going to be for – how long? It didn't make him happy. It didn't make him proud. If truth be told, it made him ashamed. But he wasn't going to admit that to anyone, least of all his father. To show a hint of weakness would make him out to be less than a man. How could he live up to his brother – the golden boy. Popular, everyone's mate, in employment, now with a wife, a future. What did his future hold? More of the same. 'Feckless!' was a word he'd heard the mother of one of his mates shout at her son, 'Good fer nuthing!' Might as well be him she was describing. His mate just laughed and made some rude gesture at her behind her back while flinging his other arm around Amos' shoulders and heading off to the pub.

The only place Amos had felt secure, had felt that he had a place and a reason to get up in the morning was when he was in the bloody army! Good God! The realisation of it hit him like a blow to the solar plexus. The bloody army! What a joke! He had hated every minute of it. Obeying pointless orders. Marching back and forth just to fill the time and keep the drill sergeant happy. Slogging through mud and worse, just to get back to camp and eat the army rations and get a bit of kip. And what did he get out of it all? Caught the bloody clap. That's about all he did come back with! And yet... And yet there was camaraderie, security, order, routine, no need to make plans – someone else did that for you, didn't need to think, just obey orders, today, tomorrow, next week, next month...

Sod it! He sat up, feeling he had been hit square on the jaw with the realisation of it all. He knew what he had to. Dragging his old kit bag from under the bed, he threw his army boots into the bottom of it, then collected a few other items which he rolled up and added, crept into the bathroom and picked up his razor, shaving gear and his toothbrush and stuffed it into a towel which he rolled up and added to the bag. Collecting his tobacco tin and a few last personal items, he threw his old army jacket over his shoulder and silently opened the door, headed down the stairs, all the while listening for the approach of any of the family. But from the sound of it they were all enjoying the last of the balmy evening air out in the garden and were unaware of either his arrival or departure. There was a fluttering in his abdomen but whether it was fear or relief, he didn't know. What he did know was that this was the only way ahead for him.

CHAPTER THIRTY-SEVEN

Lincoln 2018

After the tea break Sue and Harry returned to the pile of papers of Amos Davis' military record. Was there no end to it? Sue felt sick to her stomach after she had read what Amos' job had been in 1919. But the records didn't end there. Bit by bit they sorted the remaining paperwork into some sort of chronological order and from it started to piece together the next part of Amos' time in the Army. Sue began noting down the next important dates.

12 June 1920 – Signed on for ... years. 4th East Yorks

"I can't make this out Harry, can you?" Sue asked. They bent their heads over the blotched and blurry record but neither could finally agree on the number of years. However she could see that again his particulars were given.

Height: 5'6 ¼", Weight: 112lb, Girth: 34 ½ ". Fresh complexion, grey eyes, dark hair, C of E.

23 June 1920 – posted – Leicestershire Regiment of Foot; 23 June posted – depot

"Oh dear, that didn't last long," sighed Sue after a few minutes scrutinising the next few lines. "Look," and she pointed to the next entry.

9th September 1920 – private; drunk on defaulters roll call at 21.30h; admonished.

Sue continued scanning down the entries and the same words were repeated again and again – *drunk, absent, defaulter, punishment, detention...* And the punishments and fines increased over the months and years.

Fined 2/6d. Fined 10/=, forfeit one day's pay.

"This just gets worse," sighed Sue. "What a picture it paints."

December 1921 – absent from tattoo until 23.25h; drunk on return to barracks, using abusive language to Sergeant Brown.

April 1922- posted to Athlone; issued with one pair of foot supports.

November 1922 – breaking out of barracks (Section 10 (4) AA). Punishment 84 days imprisonment.

March 1923 – under arrest awaiting trial by DEM.

May 1923 – to be discharged with ignominy from HM Service for (i) breaking out of barracks and (ii) using threatening language to his superior officer.

July 1923 – to Military Prison, Woking

September 1923 – discharged under Kings Regulations 392 (xiii) – which is 'Having been sentenced to be discharged with ignominy'; Sect. 8(2C) AA Lichfield 25 September '23.

Sue sat back, her hands over her face. "This is just awful," she whispered. "Poor boy."

Harry stretched out a hand and laid it on her arm. "I fear it's only one of many such instances."

"But it's so unfair. He needed help and understanding. No young lad should have had to go through what he did!" Sue shook her head and smiled apologetically as the other members of the class turned and looked in her direction at her raised voice.

"I imagine today he would have had counselling and perhaps we would call it some form of PTSD. But things were very different then. He was only one of thousands who came back damaged, not physically but invisibly – mentally. You've heard of shell shock? At least people could see some evidence of their troubled mind. But for others it was completely hidden – until they went off the rails like your young chap."

"Do you know, I've got such a feeling of wanting to be able to go back and support him. And he isn't even our family, he's just my grandmother's step-brother. In fact not even that; they shared no blood. Oh my, this family history research can really dig up some stuff, can't it?" Sue sat back feeling exhausted. "I think I've had enough for one night. I think I'll head off."

As she collected all her paperwork and packed up her laptop, Harry sat up and stretched. "Me too," he said. "Walk you to your car?"

"Thanks," smiled Sue. "You've been a great help this evening. Thank you."

Later that evening, as Sue sat cradling a strong cup of coffee on her battered sofa, she revisited the facts about Amos and felt a chill descend on her. Something worried her about Amos. She shouldn't have any connection to him at all. No DNA. No blood relative. But yet something was niggling at her and she felt that there was a missing piece of the puzzle here. She couldn't explain that feeling of foreboding that hung over her. The ticking of the hall clock filled the silence of the cottage and she suddenly felt uncomfortable. How could that possibly be? This old ramshackle, battered, comfy old cottage had been her home for ever. It was a friend, a haven, a refuge.

With a harrumph she stood and switched on the old television in the corner and the room was filled with raucous canned laughter from an inane comedy programme, but she didn't care. "Silly old woman!" she remonstrated with herself. And grabbing her mobile phone she dialled her granddaughter Kate's number and sat back on the sofa as Rosie the cat curled up on her lap and all was well with the world again.

CHAPTER THIRTY-EIGHT

October 1923 York

The autumn leaves were blowing down Granby Road as Amos walked slowly along in the evening dusk, his kit bag slung over one shoulder, his army cap barely covering his closely cropped hair. He had thought twice about writing ahead but in the end, he had scribbled a hasty note and sent it from Woking where he had been imprisoned. He hadn't given much in the way of information; in fact he had barely been in touch with the family since he had crept out of the house and re-enlisted over three years ago. A postcard from Dublin. A Christmas card one year when he was feeling festive under the influence of some port wine. He hadn't left a forwarding address so he didn't know what would greet him when he arrived back home. Did they still even live here? He didn't know. If he felt shame, he wasn't about to show it, or explain where he had been or what he had done.

But in the long, lonely nights in the chilly army prison cell he went over and over the intervening years. The day he had first enlisted in 1917, full of bravado and determined to be as good as his brother, do his bit, be a hero. Instead the Army used him and others like him as human excavators. Discipline was the only comfort. Obey and you're welcomed into the whole bloody family, with the ranks above you judging you every day. But don't fall out of line. Don't fight back, even if it's the only way you know how to survive. Conform. Obey. Don't think for yourself. Don't think. Just do. Don't question. Don't try to reason. Just obey. Work. March. Sleep. Eat. Obey. Repeat. But when the demons come... What do you do then? Pick a fight with someone – anyone, just so you can hit out at something. Drink till you can't hear or see them any longer. Bugger them all! And then you're on a charge – again.

Then one day, realisation came in the form of a crushed and crumpled letter. It had followed him around and God knows how it had found him. It had been written many months before but it was from Kate. She had written to let him know he had become an uncle. James and Ethel had had a little boy and he was to be named John Samuel Amos Davis. When he saw it, his eyes filled with tears. How could they possibly want to name an innocent babe after a drink-sodden, feckless bastard like him? It struck at his very core – a place well-hidden over the years. And in the loneliness of that prison cell, on a cold dark night he sobbed, like he had never sobbed before, until his ribs ached and he felt he had nothing left to cry with anymore. For all the poor sods he had dug up, for all the officers he had sworn at, the men he had fought with, the women he had spent a meaningless night with – but most of all for himself. For the person he had left behind long ago. For the person he had become. For the dark cloak he couldn't shake off.

*****

He stood at the front door, hesitating. Everything looked the same. The black and white tiled path, the wooden door with the lion-head knocker, the half-drawn curtains at the parlour window. From within a faint glow shone through the pane of glass above the door, no doubt coming from the kitchen along the corridor. Swallowing hard, he rapped the knocker and stood back, ready to apologise to the stranger who might answer. It seemed an eternity until he could hear a shuffling behind the door and the door handle being turned.

Silhouetted in the glow stood Kate, peering around the half-open door, trying to see who would be at the door at this hour. They both stood frozen for a moment, unsure of what to say or who should make the first move but it was Kate whose face broke into a smile and stretched forth her arms to welcome him in. Pushing him ahead of her, he came though the kitchen door to find his father in his usual chair at the table, rolling a cigarette. A pile of sewing had been abandoned in the rocking chair by the range, a sewing box open on the small table beside it. The domesticity of it almost overwhelmed him after the cold brutality of his last billet. His father stood awkwardly and then stretched out his hand and grasped it firmly.

"Welcome 'ome, lad. Tis reet good t'see thee."

"Yes, yes!" Kate joined in, putting her arms around his shoulders and propelling him towards an empty chair. "Sit down. I'll put the kettle on. Oh, it's so good to see you. Where ..." but then she let the words fall, thinking better of bombarding him with questions.

Over the next half hour tea was drunk, bread was spread with butter and jam, the range was stoked up and news was shared. Amos learned about James and Ethel and thanked Kate for sending him the news of the birth of their son. He discovered he would soon be an uncle again, certainly before Christmas. Lizzie was still working at the factory. Bert's sister had died right at the end of the Spanish Flu epidemic. But Amos shared little, saying noncommittally that his period of enlistment had finished and that he wouldn't be going back to the Army. He skimmed over where he had been, merely saying that he had been in Dublin at one point and told them of the dreadful crossing by boat over the Irish Sea one stormy night.

But as the conversation started to flag, Kate said that she would go upstairs and make up his bed in his old room and leave him some blankets and towels. A few minutes later Amos gratefully climbed the stairs and shutting the bedroom door behind him, sank down on the bed hearing the familiar squeak of the springs, and sat with his head in his hands. He was home. But now what? His options were few and his plans as yet unmade.

*****

The days and weeks passed, settling back into the familiar

rhythm that Amos had missed yet had railed against. James had come round the next day when he heard his brother was back and said he'd look out for any jobs going that might suit him. In the end he got a job at the Rowntrees factory as a storeman, which basically meant packing and stacking the confectionery in boxes ready for shipping around the country. Lizzie was thrilled to have her brother back home and they often would walk back home together in the evening with a few of Lizzie's friends. It all seemed incredibly dull to Amos and yet he was warm, fed, had money to his name and had a comfortable place to lay his head at night. It should make him deliriously happy, he thought ruefully. But there was another side to him, another part that he shared with no-one. An itch he needed to scratch. A fight he needed to have.

As Christmas approached, the family welcomed James and Ethel's second child, a daughter named Frances Eileen Eliza Davis. The following afternoon James and his brother went to wet the baby's head at the local pub and as the hours passed, Amos sank back into the comfortable haze of insensibility. James walked him home, being by far the more sober of the two. Helping him into the house, he lay his brother on his bed and clattered back down the stairs and out of the door, preparing himself to face Ethel's remonstrations at the late hour of his return.

The hum of voices from downstairs broke through his half-sleep and he soon heard the familiar light fast footsteps of Lizzie coming up to her room. Amos lay thinking thoughts that he couldn't share with anyone.

*****

One Sunday morning, as everyone was getting ready for church, Kate had picked up a bundle of ironing she had finished and folded the night before and was heading up the stairs to stack the freshly laundered sheets in the linen press on the landing. She had only gone up two or three stairs when she was aware of someone at the end of the landing. Only Amos and Lizzie were inside, and she knew that Bert was out in the yard polishing his shoes as she had seen him through the kitchen window before heading upstairs. Looking upward as she mounted the next couple of stairs, she was able to make out the shadowy crouched figure of Amos hovering at Lizzie's bedroom door. At the sound of her footsteps, he straightened up and jumped back, turning to see her reaching the top of the stairs with the ironing.

"Gimme that. Lemme help 'ee," he offered, and she gladly handed the pile over to his outstretched arms.

"Time to get going to church, Amos. Are you ready? Give Lizzie a call for me, won't you? I'll just get my hat and I'll meet you both downstairs," and with that she went into the bedroom, closing the door behind her.

It was only as she sat down on the stool in front of her dressing table mirror and pushed a few stray hairs back in place that she revisited in her mind the scene she had just stumbled upon. She was sure Amos had been crouched down at Lizzie's bedroom door, just level with the keyhole. Surely not? She dismissed the thought, but a momentary shadow flitted across her mind.

Church was an occasion to catch up with neighbours, and the latest gossip. As couples and family groups dispersed, the disparate groups made their different ways home, savouring the thought of Sunday lunch and enjoying the sunshine. Kate walked with her next-door neighbour, a woman of similar age who had lost two of her three sons in the Great War. Her husband was already deep in conversation with Bert as they discussed their respective vegetable plots. Kate looked round and expected to see Lizzie not far behind, but instead she caught sight of her and Amos walking together, apart from the others. Lizzie was laughing at something Amos was saying, and he was bending close to share some comment he didn't want to be heard by the passers-by. As he did so, Kate saw him slip his arm around Lizzie's back and pull her closer, leaving his arm there around her waist. Kate shivered, even though the sun was pleasantly warm upon her shoulders. Normally she would never have given it another thought, but something made her keep her gaze upon them. Only her neighbour's hand upon her arm, and her repeated question, made her turn away and carry on homeward, but she did so with heavy steps.

*****

He could be so charming. Those deep dark eyes of his could draw you in. And he could tell stories of such exciting things and places he'd been. Sometimes she wondered if they were all true, but in the end it didn't matter. He could make her laugh and he was much more interesting than the other factory lads who mooned at her, wolf-whistled or blushed when she spoke to them. The other girls must envy her. Amos was stronger and better built than all those puny chaps that tried to catch her eye.

Soon it was just the two of them walking home in the winter dark. He was so attentive, making sure she was warm enough when they detoured through the park on the way home. He'd wrap his arms around her and then envelope them both in his thick coat left over from his Army days. They'd find a seat sometimes, out of sight of passersby and he'd hold her close. She never felt uncomfortable, then. But the first time he tried to kiss her, she pulled away.

"Amos, s'not right. You're my brother!"

"Ah, but that's where you're wrong, little 'un. Ah'm not even yer 'alf-brother. Didn't 'ee know?" and he continued to explain that her mother wasn't his mother, nor her father his. At first, she didn't believe him. She knew that Bert was widowed when they'd married but had just always assumed that he was her father.

"How d'you know?" she challenged him.

"Ah heard 'em talkin' once, years ago. Me dad said that day would've been our mother's birthday and Kate said that 'er husband's would 'ave been the week before, just before you were born. They started talkin' a bit more but then they must 'ave 'eard me and shut the door."

He stopped and let Lizzie take in the import of what he had just said.

"So – ye see, we're not even blood," and he paused to let that sink in, then let his fingers stroke the back of her neck while he moved closer.

*****

It felt good to touch soft skin again, to feel the swell of a soft body under his hands. She was so trusting. She wasn't experienced in those ways that the sluts around the Army camps were. And in a way that made it all the more intoxicating. He knew he'd have to take it slowly or else he'd scare her off. The information he'd given her was a stroke of genius. And after all, it was true, but it had shaken her and so it was to him she looked for support and understanding. They could talk about it. They could share the common feeling of being children of other parents. Of being half-related but not related. And, he assured her, that was probably why they were drawn to each other, sought comfort in each other's company.

*****

But Kate was not blind to what was happening. She didn't feel she could talk about it to Bert. He was just so grateful to have his son home again, but Kate had a responsibility to her own daughter, her own flesh and blood. She spent sleepless nights, her ears straining for any movement on the landing outside their bedrooms.

As she sat unfolding a letter with payment from one of her

customers, she opened her writing slope and drew out her pen and the small notebook in which she listed payments and orders. Sweeping her hand over the smooth leather reminded her of the first time she had been given it by Uncle Charles and how thrilled she had been. Within it she stored stamps and envelopes, notepaper and string, sealing wax and a small penknife – all the accoutrements required for correspondence. As she replaced the notebook, she ran her hands down the smooth edges and sat back with a sigh. The house was quiet, she was alone but soon she would need to prepare the evening meal as everyone would come home hungry after a busy day at work. The tick of the hall clock measured the rhythm of her thoughts. She revisited the years in between, the twists and turns of fate that had brought her to where she was now. The happy times and the sad. The fears and the joys. Now nearly fifty, her hair was streaked with silver strands, lines measured the weight of smiles and frowns, her figure, though still shapely had required some judicious reshaping of skirts and bodices.

Her thoughts turned to her brother Henry and her tiny baby, both taken far too young. Perhaps naming the babe after his uncle was ill-fated. Her fingers strayed unbidden to the secret catch and explored the cavity beneath. The hard edges of the cockle shell cradled next to the downy softness of the lock of hair, not quite dark and not quite fair, not quite wavy but not quite straight. As she lay the shell in her palm, memories crowded in and her eyes grew heavy with the tears about to be shed. And now another child needed her protection. A heavy weight lay in the pit of her stomach when she realised what must be done and her fingers curled around the shell, the sharp edges digging into the skin of her hand.

CHAPTER THIRTY-NINE

February 2019 York

Her university tutor handed out details of the second year module and gave them the link to the list of sources they could use. Slapping down the lid of her laptop, Kate slid it into her bag and slung it over her shoulder. Part of what she wanted to do was to explore the link between primary and secondary sources relating to the outbreak and spread of the Spanish Flu in York in the couple of years after the end of World War I. She would start trawling through what was available online when she got back to the flat, she decided, but dodged into the local Costa to grab a latte and a filled baguette to sustain her through the afternoon.

As she closed the front door, she felt the vibration of her phone in the back pocket of her jeans. Balancing the latte on the edge of the nearest free surface and dropping everything else to the floor, she reached around behind her and smiled as she saw who the caller was.

"Hi Gran! How are you?"

"Hi Kate! Hope things are OK with you? Are you busy?"

"Not at the moment, just in actually and about to grab a bite to eat. Everything OK?"

"Oh yes, all's well," Gran replied, followed by some muffled shuffling and a muted voice saying, "Get down puss!" After another load of scrabbling around, Gran resumed her conversation. "Sorry, that was Rosie. She wouldn't get off my lap and I wanted to reach some papers on the coffee table. Now, I've a wee favour to ask you."

"No problem, go ahead. What is it?" Kate asked, at the same time trying to relocate the latte cup to a safer spot.

"I've been doing some more family research and I've been finding some amazing stuff. But a lot of it happens in York and I wondered if you know if there's anywhere local to you that would have more information. According to the tutor, some stuff hasn't been digitised yet and needs researching in person, or by paying a researcher. I just wondered ..."

They spent the next few minutes discussing what Gran wanted to find and Kate explaining where she might be able to find it. In fact, following on from what she needed to do for her assignment, it all might link up quite well. By the time Gran had gone off at a tangent about her latest craft project using dried seaweed and broken ceramic tiles, Kate's latte was lukewarm and her stomach was groaning in protest.

"Look, I've got to go Gran. I'll get back to you with anything I find. Lots of love!" and with that she started to unwrap the baguette and tear off a chunk, stuffing it into her mouth. Shoving the tepid latte into the microwave, she grabbed a plate from the drainer and unceremoniously dumped the baguette on to it, grimacing as a soggy slice of tomato escaped with a scattering of grated cheese.

Later, when her stomach was full and her coffee cup emptied of the frothy dregs of milk, she spread her paperwork out on the desk in her room and started to organise what she needed to do. Her eyes strayed to the incongruously dark wood of the writing slope, sitting on the bright white of the flat-pack unit. Her hands strayed there, almost without her thinking and again she revelled in the smoothness of the tapered edges and the brass escutcheon. Clicking open the secret compartment, she ran her thumbnail along the sharply serrated edge of the cockle shell and listened to the rhythmic sound it made. Laying it in her palm, her eyes grew heavy and she found herself experiencing the now-familiar lurch in her stomach.

CHAPTER FORTY

February 1924 York

In the end it had been easy. She didn't know what to expect but when he started to become more insistent, her body yielded to his and before she was aware of it, he'd had what he wanted. There was a moment when she even smiled at him, didn't want him to stop, but then realisation of what was about to happen had become clear to her and she tried to resist, making him all the more determined, assuring her it was alright, keeping her quiet, pinning her down. He just made her keep her eyes fixed on his, daring her to tear them away, holding her captive, bound for those moments while he needed her compliance – or not. In the end, it wouldn't matter. But she obeyed him, believing all the honeyed words and convincing arguments. Just to get to this moment. God, it had taken weeks to get to this point. But it was worth it. Better than all the whores he'd bedded along the way. With a grin he thought to himself, he might have even given her something else to remind her of him.

But now she was all weepy and full of remorse. Did he love her? What if their parents found out? Was it safe? It would be alright wouldn't it – she didn't know about such things. Of course, he reassured her. He knew what he was doing. It was perfectly alright. And yes, of course he cared for her. He wouldn't have done this if he hadn't, he reassured her.

But something niggled him. The look Kate had given him this morning at breakfast. The way he kept seeing her look over her shoulder at him when no-one else was around. Did she suspect? He brushed away that thought. He was just imagining it. A guilty conscience, he laughed to himself.

THE RIVER LOOKS AFTER ITS OWN

*****

Kate and Lizzie walked together in comparative silence. Usually Lizzie was chattering away about some nonsense or other, but today she was very quiet as she clutched at the umbrella that she tried to hold over them both. They'd been to deliver an evening gown to one of Kate's clients and as she also had a hat to deliver, she'd asked Lizzie if she'd come with her to carry the cumbersome hatbox in the growing wind that was thrashing the trees about and presaging an oncoming storm.

As they were about to cross the Ouse Bridge, Kate caught sight of a familiar figure on the staithe on the other side of the river, grey and already fast flowing with flotsam being carried along at an ever-growing pace. In that instant she knew what she had to do and prayed for the strength to do it quickly before she could think better of it. Taking the umbrella from Lizzie, she held it aloft and at an angle so that the wind snatched at it, pulling at her arms and bringing her to the edge of the parapet. It was now or never. Taking a deep breath she allowed herself to overbalance and as her feet left the ground, she threw her head back and met Lizzie's terrified expression.

The cold water slammed into her, taking her breath away, pulling her under. As she rose to the surface, sucking air into her lungs, she used every ounce of it to scream for help – and to the person whose attention she needed to attract. "Amos! Amos! Help me! Help!" It sounded so puny against the roar of the river. Had he seen? She was being swept along now and if he didn't look soon, she would be beyond him. Water blinded her eyes and her water-logged clothing pulled her down again, swirling around her legs and tangling her feet. As she rose a second time, she knew it would be her last chance. "AMOS!" she screamed, the tearing pain of it scraping her throat.

And then a movement. He turned. He froze. He stood stock still. Her heart sank. And then, as if galvanised into action she saw him rip his jacket off and plunge into the swirling torrent, striking out towards her. There were two things she saw as she twined her fingers into his hair and clawed at his clothing. Two last images as she lost consciousness. His eyes wide as he felt her force him down instead of allowing him to hold her up. And then. Dear God – no! A figure had launched themselves from the parapet of the bridge where they had been standing but a few moments earlier. A flash of a maroon coat and green skirt. Lizzie! No – that was not the way it was supposed to be. No, no, no.....

*****

TRAGIC DROWNING AS STORM HITS CITY
The body of a young man later identified as Amos Davis, 25, of Granby Road, York was dragged from the water of the River Ouse downstream early yesterday morning. It was believed that he entered the water off Kings Staithe the previous afternoon to rescue two women who fell from the Ouse Bridge. Witnesses said that the man struck out bravely in an attempt to rescue the women, later described as being his mother and sister, but failed in the attempt. The public are warned yet again to abstain from entering the river when in spate as this is the fourth drowning this year.
Yorkshire Gazette 19 February 1924

CHAPTER FORTY-ONE

2018 York

Kate gasped and opened her eyes staring upwards at the ceiling and the paper lantern lampshade above her. A sharp pain in her right hand made her look down and she saw that her fingers were tightly curled around something. Forcing her stiff and aching fingers apart, she released the cockle shell from her grasp and let it fall on the carpet beside her. The feeling of nausea began to recede and with relief she realised her hair was not wet and tangled, her clothes sopping or her skin cold and wet. But then another realisation swept over her. If this was Kate, what had happened to Lizzie? The transference of anguish from one Kate to another did not dissipate and she was left feeling ungrounded, in limbo. She needed to know the answer. But first she needed a strong coffee.

Dragging herself up off the bed where she had somehow collapsed, she walked slowly through to the kitchen and snapped on the kettle. Looking at the clock she realised it was only about ten minutes since she had gone through to study in her room. Yet it felt like hours.

She needed to know the answer. But she didn't want to alert or alarm Gran. Instead she called Gran's number and after a few pleasantries asked her what she knew about her grandmother Eliza. Gran shuffled a few papers at the other end of the line then read from her notes, "She was born in 1901 and she died in 1947. She ..."

Kate interrupted, "That's fine Gran. Just wondered what her dates were. Sorry, must go. Love you," and with that she drew a sigh of relief. That answered one question but not another. How?

CHAPTER FORTY-TWO

February 1924 York

K ate lay on the riverbank, vaguely aware of the people crowded around her, staring down at her and all talking at once. As the horror of what had just happened slammed into her, she choked and gasped, spewing water out of the side of her mouth. A hand stretched out to her and gently turned her onto her side. All she could see now were legs and feet, boots and shoes, skirts... And then blackness swept over her.

The next time she regained consciousness she was being lifted up and laid on something marginally softer than the cold, hard riverbank on which she had been lain. A blanket was being wrapped around her and voices were barking orders.

"Clear the way. Stand back now. Make room."

As she was lifted and carried through the crowd she caught sight of a form on the ground, a sodden maroon coat and green skirt adhering to the slim unmoving form of a woman. Did she imagine the merest movement from the inert form? Her heart leapt with a tiny flame of hope.

The last sound she heard was barely audible – a swishing, whispering sound.

Never fear.
I am always here for you.
The river looks after its own.

*****

Kate sat by the bedside, her head bent over a buttonhole she was sewing. Her ears were attuned to the sound of shallow, rhythmic breathing. She looked so pale and slight, bundled up with bedclothes, her head propped up with a cloud of pillows. She had been sitting here all day, barely leaving Lizzie's side, only accepting a cup of tea when Bert climbed the stairs and left it on the bedside table for her. It still lay there, cold and untouched with a stale film of milk across the surface. Lizzie stirred and immediately Kate sat forward, her sewing laid aside.

"I'm here. It's alright," she whispered, laying her hand over the coverlet and feeling the slight form beneath. "Do you want anything? A drink?"

Lizzie's eyelids fluttered and she took a moment to fully focus on her mother in the gloom of the curtained bedroom.

"Ma? Why am I here?' her voice so weak that Kate had to lean close to be sure of catching her words.

"You're fine now. I thought I had lost you. After spending a night at the hospital, they let you come home but then you developed pneumonia. The doctor's been coming twice a day to check on you but he's assured us you're over the worst and you just need to get your strength back. Then you'll be right as rain," and with that she managed a weak smile while she stroked her daughter's cheek. "Are you hungry? Let me get you some soup. Or tea?"

Lizzie nodded weakly and Kate stood, stretching her out the stiffness from sitting hunched so long. Giving her a reassuring smile, she quietly slipped out of the room and headed down to the kitchen.

Over the next few hours, in between slipping back and forth in and out of sleep, Lizzie started to try to piece together the fragments of memories she could grasp. She remembered the shock of the water. Then she remembered how she had ended up there, fearing for her mother – and the brother, the man she once thought had cared about her. Eventually she screwed up the courage to ask the question that now was forming in her mind.

"Amos?"

Kate turned away and let her gaze follow the flight of a flock of pigeons as they took to the air outside the window. She let the question hang in the air as long as she could before she turned back to meet Lizzie's enquiring gaze. She didn't need to speak. Lizzie could read her expression. She drew in a gasp and buried her face in her hands; the only words she could utter were "No, no, no..."

*****

Over the next few hours Lizzie revisited the scene on the bridge, the wind and rain, the cold, the sight of Amos and his reaction. And she could hear her mother's cries. Not just for help, but for Amos. And how had she cowped over the parapet? That puzzled her. Yes, of course, the umbrella. But she'd been holding it hadn't she, not her mother? A thought came to her, like a slithering snake, insinuating itself into her scraps of memory. She pushed it away, then went back and tried to grasp it again, time and time again, not wanting to admit what it was showing her, but unwilling to set it free. Eventually she held it in a place deep and close to her and said no more about the events of that day.

What she did begin to appreciate with a creeping sense of relief was that she would never have to look at his face again or fear his hands upon her, his mouth whispering in her ear while his weight pinned her down. Torn between loss for the person she had come to call brother, and the person who robbed her of her innocence in a way that brooked no resistance, she struggled to handle the weight of emotions that swept over her.

But Lizzie was not the only person who Kate had to support. Bert was a broken man. He'd had two sons join up, and two return unscathed, then to see Amos become a stranger to him, not the boy that he'd bade farewell to, instead a cold and distant man. He hid things behind those dark eyes, hooded beneath their brooding brows. Only in quiet moments did Bert admit to himself that the man who returned was unknown to him. Bert held his feelings about his son close, never sharing his misgivings with Kate. Maybe he should have. He wished he'd said some things, talked to the lad when he had the chance. Now it was too late. The best he could do was to stand at the graveside where his first wife, his infant children and now his youngest son lay cold and still and ask for forgiveness, or the ability to understand. But every time he came away with a heavy heart and no answer to the repeated question. Why...?

CHAPTER FORTY-THREE

April 2019 York

Kate grabbed her laptop and stuffed it into its bag, then clutching at the keys on the hall table she flew through the front door, letting it slam behind her. She didn't want to be late but had got distracted by a FaceTime session with one of her mates which had gone on longer than she had realised. Man trouble! After spending quite some time commiserating with Vicky while she sniffled through what seemed like a whole box of tissues, Kate eventually wound up the conversation as quickly as she could without sounding callous and promised to come over that evening, armed with a bottle of wine.

She reached the gates of the cemetery on the outskirts of the city only a couple of minutes late, but red-faced and out of breath, having pedalled hard all the way. She had learned that the fastest way to travel through York was by bike and so she and her flatmate had managed to source a second-hand one, which they used when necessary. By the gates stood an older chap, greying hair and a beard – she guessed it must be Derek, the man she'd arranged to meet. He turned to acknowledge her arrival and broke into a smile as she apologised for her lateness, assuring her that he'd only just arrived himself.

As he ushered her through the wrought iron gates and showed her where she could leave her bike, he clarified the topic of her enquiry. She told him again that she was looking at how the citizens of York had been affected by the Spanish Flu and wanted to get an idea of how many had died and the spread of ages, etc. She had discovered that fifty-nine of York's citizens had died of the flu in 1919 and hoped to focus her research on some of those. She still needed to trawl through the online records and visit the record office in person to follow up individual cases through newspaper death announcements, etc. but just being able to have a walk around the cemetery and get a feel for their final resting places would help her build up a picture and lend a dimension to her research.

Over the next hour or so, Derek took her around the cemetery, pointing out various monuments of interest, memorials and inscriptions. He gave her a potted history of the cemetery's inception and development over the last century and a half and answered her questions at length and with the kind of detail that impressed her. She switched her phone on to record while they walked when there was a particular piece of noteworthy information she would want to recall later. Eventually, he left her near the entrance and asked her to contact him if she needed any further help.

She still had most of the afternoon ahead of her so she started to stroll back round the paths, stopping every now and then to read an inscription or note a date and enjoying the peace and quiet. There were a few people around and, in the distance, a sombre group were standing in a huddle as someone dear to them was laid to rest. Not wishing to intrude, Kate struck off in the opposite direction and found herself in a more overgrown area of the cemetery. It occurred to her that she hadn't even considered if any of her ancestors might be laid to rest here. After all, up until Gran had started her research, she hadn't even been aware of any connection to York. Did she want to know? Did she want to find their names engraved in stone? She wasn't sure but thought that she might contact Derek again and see if he could locate anything significant in the cemetery records. And she thought, she might even bring a posy to lay on their grave – that would be a nice thing to do, and she'd send a picture to Gran to add to her file of research.

She sat down on a bench set back in the shade of some rhododendron bushes and clicked on her phone recording, tucking her Bluetooth buds into her ears. Scribbling down a list of points of note and further areas of research she wished to follow up, she passed another hour and so, and it was only as she became aware of the chill air that she noted the time. A thrush regaled her with its melodious song, before scuffling through the undergrowth in search of snail shells to hammer open. The leaves above her trembled as a squirrel balanced along a branch and then acrobatically jumped across the gap to the next tree.

The dark shapes of the headstones, some upright, some lopsided, looked like a parade of drunken revellers, knee-deep in the longer shadowy grass. If only they could talk, she mused. But then again, perhaps not – and with a shiver she stood and packed up her stuff and headed back into the sunshine and onto the path leading to the entrance gates.

CHAPTER FORTY-FOUR

May 1924 York

Lizzie had recovered physically but she seemed to have lost her love of life and her ebullience; her infectious laughter was never heard and she often stayed in her room rather than sit in the kitchen chatting after meals. In the intervening months, Kate had tried to assure herself that her daughter would soon recover and encouraged her to meet up with friends, go to the music hall or join the choir group cycling off after church for outings to the countryside. But it became evident that Lizzie had something locked inside her that she wouldn't, or couldn't, share. Lizzie hadn't given her any of her monthly rags to soak and boil wash for her. She was pale and drawn and avoiding everyone – family and friends. It felt like a cold hand had grabbed her heart as Kate pieced together the evidence and knew that she needed to have that conversation with her daughter.

She chose a warm Saturday afternoon when Bert had gone to the cemetery to tidy up Amos' grave and sit for a while, which he did most weekends. Calling Lizzie into the kitchen, she put a cup of tea in front of her and swallowed hard, thinking how to broach the subject. After a few minutes of uncomfortable silence stretched out between them, Kate turned and took a deep breath as she pulled out a chair and sat across the table from her. But it was Lizzie who broke the silence, letting out a deep sob and hiding her face in her hands. Her only words were, "Oh Ma!..."

Kate stood and enveloped her in her arms, letting her sob until she was exhausted. All she said was, "I know, my pet. I know. It's alright, we'll get through this."

Kate didn't know how she could begin to tell Bert but, in the end, an opportunity arose and seemed a kind of solution, a way forward. Bert had been reading the paper a few days later and left it folded on his chair, rising to go outside and sit for a while with his pipe, enjoying the last rays of the evening sun after a busy day. These days his bones ached after a heavy day's digging and his knees were not as good as they used to be. But he had a few good years in him yet, he mused.

Kate started to tidy up the plates and dry them, setting out the table ready for breakfast. Tutting, she lifted the newspaper Bert had been reading and went to add it to the basket by the fire, ready to use as kindling to start the stove in the morning, when she noticed Bert had circled an item in the Wanted section.

WANTED: experienced gardener/groundsman for 6 acre garden and grounds 5 miles from Lincoln. Experience of vegetable and fruit cultivation as well as more formal garden management will be essential. Responsibility for managing a team of 2 under-gardeners. Position comes with rent-free tenancy of a tied cottage. Applicants will need to show references and present themselves for interview at the end of the month. Applications in writing to Lord Barwell, Skelthorpe Hall, Lincoln.

Kate was dumbstruck, unsure of whether Bert was seriously considering this. Or maybe it was for a friend, or maybe even James. But no, the position would suit him to a tee. And as she let her mind wander, she began to see that such a move would solve quite a few other problems.

Unsure how to broach the topic, she unfolded the paper and laid it out on the table tucked under the cup and saucer he would use for breakfast, the circled advertisement in full view, in the hope he would realise she had seen it.

"That's me going up now Bert. Will you lock up? Mind and leave me those socks of yours to darn," and with that she headed up to bed.

*****

A week later Kate walked down to the station and met Bert off the Lincoln train. Never one to give much away, she tried to read his expression but he wasn't going to talk about it until he'd had a cup of tea and got his boots off and sat by his own fireside.

Eventually she dragged the details from him, his interview and the questions he'd had to answer. He wouldn't be told the outcome until the end of the week – this was Wednesday – so she'd have to be patient. Had he been shown the cottage, she asked, but he said no, he hadn't although he had been told it had two bedrooms, a parlour and kitchen, with an added outhouse which had recently been fitted with a bath and lavatory. "Well," Kate said, "I suppose that will do."

The letter arrived second post on Saturday afternoon and by that evening the move to Lincoln was their only topic of conversation. Kate could see that Bert was proud that he'd been given the position, having since found out that four other applicants had been in the running. But now she knew she had to talk to him about Lizzie and why this move was actually the answer to her prayers. She found it hard to find the words to tell him of Lizzie's condition but in the end, after the 'what', she couldn't bear to also tell him the 'how' and the 'who'. He was so disappointed that Lizzie had got herself in this condition and wanted to make the lad in question face up to his responsibilities. For once, though, Kate asserted herself as Lizzie's mother, reminding him he was not Lizzie's blood relative, and as such she and Lizzie had decided not to name the father for reasons they had both agreed upon. Bert was about to rail against their decision but the look Kate gave him brooked no argument. So – a move away from York, from everyone who knew them, a fresh start – that was a fortuitous outcome for them all.

CHAPTER FORTY-FIVE

April 2019 York

On a whim, Kate had asked Derek if he could find the resting place of her Hoxton ancestors, hoping that she could surprise Gran with an added piece of information to add to her growing family file. And so this cold, damp Saturday morning when she should be snuggled up in bed, here she was instead, hair frizzy after her cycle ride in the drizzling rain, leaving her cycle and helmet and setting off through the mist to locate the whereabouts of the grave marked on the cemetery plan. Thankfully she'd had the presence of mind to put it in a plastic wallet otherwise it would be sodden in no time. At first, she couldn't orientate herself and spent a few moments trying to find a point of reference to strike out from, but eventually she recognised the layout of paths and headed off to the older part of the cemetery.

Here the grass was longer and the undergrowth more tangled. Gauzy ribbons of mist swirled about as she brushed through the fallen leaves. The trail she was following became more indistinct and she fought to shake of the sense of being watched by many pairs of unseen eyes, hidden in the dripping bushes and shrubs that blocked her way. All the colours were muted and blended into one sombre hue, giving the scene the sense of being an old and faded black and white photograph. Stopping to check the worn and faded names on the headstones as she neared the spot indicated with a red circle on the plan, she struggled to make them out and wondered if she'd actually manage to locate it or had she missed it completely?

Stopping to reorientate herself, she took a minute to pause and look around. It seemed that she was the only person here this murky morning. 'I hope Gran appreciates this,' she thought ruefully. The scuffling of some small creature in the undergrowth startled her and she swung round to try to locate the source. But instead, there it was. The stone dark and damp, the lettering still deeply cut and legible despite the century or more since it had been cut. She stepped closer and knelt down, squinting at the names and dates.

> *William Hoxton died 20th December 1882,*
> *and his dearly beloved wife Elizabeth died 2nd Feb 1872*
> *Also in memory of his second wife Laura Emily*
> *and her son Henry Shipton, both drowned*
> *22nd December 1882 at Naburn Lock.*
> *Safe in the Arms of Jesus*

Kate scrabbled in her jeans pocket for her phone and crouched down to take a picture of it, then a couple more from different angles, with and without the flash, until she was happy that most of the detail could be seen clearly. Stepping backwards to try to get a shot showing more of the setting, she stumbled over the edge of another plot and promptly found herself sitting on the damp ground. Within seconds, her bottom was becoming sodden and she struggled to stand before she was completely soaked through. Turning to look at the offending grave, she squinted at the name, about to remonstrate with the incumbent for causing her soaked behind. It was of similar size and stone to that of her ancestors' headstone but she had to squint until she could make out the inscription.

> *In loving memory of*
> *Frances Ann Davis died 3rd May 1899,*
> *also her daughter Sarah Mary,*
> *aged 5 days old 9th July 1897*
> *and her husband Herbert John Davis*
> *died 17th September 1938, aged 68*
> *Also his baby son Henry Charles Davis,*
> *aged 3 days old 24th April 1905*

Also his son Amos Henry Davis
drowned 24th February 1924.

"Well, I don't know who you are but thanks for introducing yourself!" she muttered. As she turned to collect her phone, which had fallen out of her hand beside her, she could have sworn she heard a deep, mocking laugh and swivelling her head around, she tried to locate who had been within earshot – if indeed there was anyone. But even through the silvery mist of drizzle she could see that she was quite alone.

By the time she had retraced her steps and collected her bike, she had convinced herself that her imagination had been playing tricks on her, but she couldn't shake off the feeling that there had been some significance in the fact that the two graves were beside each other. And that the second had pointedly attracted her attention!

*****

Gran was thrilled with the new information that Kate sent her by way of a photograph in a text message later that day. But not before Kate had stripped off her soaking jeans and dived into a hot shower, drying and straightening her hair and curling up on the couch with a hot chocolate. The phone buzzed, indicating a reply from Gran and Kate laughed at the WOW! emoji Gran had sent. Seconds later the phone rang and Gran's voice bubbled down the phone with excitement. A few minutes later, Kate told her of the soaked bottom escapade, and Gran fell about laughing, saying she wished she'd had a picture of that!

"I've a couple more of the headstone, some close ups. Hang on, I'll send them," and opening her photos, she pressed select on the remaining images and pressed send.

All was quiet for a minute or so as Gran received and looked at the remaining photos.

"What's that last blurry one? Looks like a different headstone to the Hoxton one?"

"No, they're all the same one," Kate replied, looking more closely at the photos she had sent. But the last one was a different headstone, slightly blurred and at a tilted angle.

"That's really spooky. I had to zoom in to the photo a bit. How did you know I had found out about Amos Davis? He was your three times great grandmother's husband's son by his first marriage. He had a sad life. I got a bit sidetracked by him and his war record. But he's not directly related to us."

But all that evening Kate couldn't help feeling there was something she was missing. It niggled at her, but in the end she shook it off and settled down with her flatmate Jen to watch a movie on Netflix.

CHAPTER FORTY-SIX

June 1925, Cranfield Cottage, Skelthorpe, Near Lincoln

Today marked a year since they had moved from York to the stone cottage by the gates of Skelthorpe Hall. Bert had become a well-respected member of the outdoor staff and one to whom her Ladyship sent her requests for cut flowers to grace the house or for dinner parties, and to whom Cook sent the scullery maid to collect the required vegetables and herbs from the walled kitchen garden to concoct this evening's dinner. Kate had quickly set about giving the cottage 'a good bottoming' upon their arrival, tutting and shaking her head at the state the previous incumbent had left it. Bert informed her he'd been the previous head gardener, living alone and into his eighties when he eventually passed from this life. Nevertheless, it took a week or more before the cottage smelled fresh and clean, and every surface gleamed from hours of elbow grease and beeswax and finally met her high standards.

In pride of place, on a table in the corner of the parlour, stood her writing slope, polished but slightly showing its age through years of loyal service. It held receipts and bills, treasured letters and photographs of James and Ethel's children as they grew, recipe clippings from the *Woman's Weekly* magazine and scribbled measurements on the back of an envelope for a jumper for Bert. And it held its secrets, less visited than in times past, but still offering comfort by simply knowing they were there.

As the months passed into autumn and Lizzie's time came near, Kate kept busy making baby clothes and teaching Lizzie to knit. One misty morning in November, Lizzie went into labour and a few hours later a healthy baby girl came into the world, loudly announcing her arrival. Lizzie named her Maud Kate Davis. Kate went to register the birth in Lincoln and, at Lizzie's request, left the father's name unrecorded, effectively wiping away the memory of Amos for ever more.

LINCOLN	Where and when born	Name, if any	Sex	Name and surname of father	Name, surname and maiden name of mother	Occupation of father	Signature, description and residence of informant	When registered
	Twelfth November 1924 Cranfield Cottage, Skelthorpe, Lincolnshire	Maud Katherine	F		Eliza Kate Davis		Kate E. Davis, grandmother, Cranfield Cottage, Skelthorpe	23 November 1924

*****

The years passed and Lizzie met and then married a widower, a plumber who initially came to deal with the faulty pipes up at the Hall, but then made every excuse to keep passing by the gardener's cottage to check on this or that. Kate smiled to herself when she realised what was happening when Harry kept dropping by. Eventually he popped the question and Lizzie and he were married in February of 1926 at the Register Office in Lincoln, followed by a small reception at a local pub. Harry had little twin girls from his first marriage, Alice and Violet, and they were fond of Lizzie and soon all five of them became a happy little family. Almost immediately Lizzie fell pregnant and on the fifth of November gave birth to a boy she named George Frederick. Kate and Bert loved when they all came to visit at the cottage and the children were allowed to run around the lawns which were out of sight of the Hall. Kate allowed herself to revel in being a grandmother and life seemed, at last, to have settled into a peaceful routine.

*****

A few years later, following an unseasonably damp and cold autumn, Bert developed a hacking cough and much to his displeasure, was confined to bed under orders of the local doctor. He grew weaker and was often so racked with coughing that he could not catch his breath. He slipped away one morning in

September, as the storm clouds of war were threatening over Europe.

The family travelled up to York to lay him to rest with his first wife, their baby daughter and Kate's baby son, Henry. As Kate stood at the graveside, she shivered involuntarily when she saw the name of Amos also etched upon the very bottom of the headstone. Beside her she could sense the same reaction in Lizzie, and they held each other's hand tightly in a silent gesture of unity and support.

Together the family walked back past the imposing Clifford's Tower and stopped off at a local tearoom for a late lunch. James and Ethel, who had joined them, bade their goodbyes and headed home. The children were restless after trying to be so well behaved in the cemetery so after they had eaten, they walked down by the river Ouse through a the small park. Unbidden, the memories of past times came flooding back to Kate and she had to hold on tight to Lizzie's arm. Feeling her mother's weight, Lizzie turned to see the colour drain from Kate's face. Shouting on Harry to stop, Lizzie led her mother to a bench and made her sit and catch her breath. The children were far ahead, George racing after his half-sisters, shouting and laughing, the solemnity of the funeral forgotten.

By now Kate had started shaking, then she began rocking back and forth, her mouth contorted and twisted to one side.

"Ma, Ma!" wailed Lizzie, putting her arms about her and trying to hold her up. By now Harry had joined them and said he would go and find some help. Kate was trying to speak but the words were slurred and Lizzie had to bend closer to try to make them out.

"... made me. Jus' a liddle push... Ma never knew ... was me. Henry – oh, my lil' brother. Why ... did I ... Evil ... you are. Can hear you ... now. Get 'way! ... "

Lizzie was alarmed at the garbled words her mother was uttering. Taking a handkerchief from her coat pocket, she wiped away the spittle that ran from the side of her mother's mouth.

"Hush, Ma. It's alright. Harry's gone for help. Just sit still," Lizzie comforted her. By now the children had seen something was wrong and were running back towards them. Not wanting to alarm them, Lizzie told them Gran was just tired and upset and that they should just leave her in peace till she felt better. Sending them off to collect conkers, Lizzie turned back to Kate.

She was trying to reach out her hand, but not to her daughter, instead towards the riverbank as if she was pointing at something.

"... hear you. ... can't get me now. ... gave yer two of them. ... debt's paid... Two boys in exchange ... fer me, for m' girl..."

By now Lizzie could see Harry coming with another man, running down the path towards them. The man carried a bag and Lizzie assumed he was a doctor. Kneeling down in front of Kate, the doctor felt her pulse and looked at her closely. "I think your mother may have had a stroke. It looks like she has had a shock, which is not surprising as your husband tells me you have been at your father's funeral today."

Lizzie nodded and searched the doctor's face for some better news. "I think we should get her to the hospital and get her checked over properly. Wait here, I'll phone from the hotel over there. It shouldn't take too long," he added as he stood, and headed off across the road.

"What's your mother trying to say?" asked Harry, bending closer.

"It's nothing," Lizzie replied, "she's just confused."

About ten minutes later the ringing of the ambulance's bell

could be heard approaching. By now the children were looking scared and worried and Harry tried to reassure them while Lizzie leant over Kate, stroking the back of her hand to try to comfort and calm her. As the men carried the stretcher to the waiting ambulance, she struggled to raise herself on one elbow, craning her neck in the direction of the river as it slid effortlessly past the bank, the sunlight glinting off it and the boats that passed making ripples that gently washed the staithes.

So you have returned.
It's been a long time. I have always been patient.
But of course you know that.
I would have liked to have had more time to – reminisce.
So sorry you have to go…
Always pleased to meet old friends.
I would have liked to have made the acquaintance of your family.
Oh well…. maybe one day – I can wait.
Weeks, months.
Years.
I'll always be here…

Kate fell back upon the stretcher with a gasp and everything grew dim and deathly quiet.

CHAPTER FORTY-SEVEN

June 2019 Lincoln

By now Sue had amassed quite a fat file of information which she had started to sort into sections pertaining to each branch and generation. She was also getting to be quite an expert at using her family history programme to add information and extend the tree, albeit getting side-tracked more often than not.

Now she could add the photographs of the headstone that Kate had sent her, which also filled in some information about her great grandfather Herbert and his previous marriage to Frances Burton. Such a pity there were so many illegitimate births, she mused. So many dead ends. Brick walls, her tutor called them. She certainly couldn't see how she might ever break them down.

Soon Kate would be home for the summer, her module assessments completed and at the end of her second year of study. How time flew! It seemed no time since she was a little girl, hardly aware of the tragedy surrounding her mother's death when she was barely two years old. She and Geoff had been more than happy to shoulder the responsibility of bringing up their little granddaughter, seeing her mother Debbie every day in her smile, her colouring and her gentle nature. It was lovely to hear the cottage ringing to the sound of a child's voice again. Yes, the old cottage had seen many families live under its roof. As far as she could make out, her great grandparents Kate and Herbert, with her grandmother Eliza, had moved in about 1924, and her mother Maud had been born there the same year.

Looking back over her notes, she realised she already had found the 1939 Register record of Eliza and Henry Watkins when they were living at Richmond Lane, Lincoln. So if the cottage had stayed in the family, might Kate have still been there in 1939? Sue fired up her laptop and logged in to FindMyPast entering her great grandmother's name and the address of the cottage. After a few seconds a list of possible records came up and Sue quickly found the one she needed. Under the heading for Skelthorpe was a list of addresses in the village and halfway down Cranfield Cottage jumped out from the left-hand column. Looking across, there were only two people listed as living in the cottage:

1. Watkins Kate E, Female, 11 Feb 76, W, own means
2. Watkins Violet J, Female, 23 Mar 20, S, nursing duties

The surname for Violet had been crossed out in red and the surname Sharpe added, as well as the addition of a variety of numbers and letters in the far left-hand column which meant nothing to Sue. But from what the tutor had told them about the layout of the 1939 Register, Sue could deduce that Violet was probably a relative of Kate's and most probably was looking after her. And sometime after 1939, Violet had married a man surname Sharpe. But also Violet's name had not been redacted, which implied she had died.

The sound of approaching footsteps made Sue look up in anticipation, and sure enough the scrape of the front door opening heralded Kate's arrival, laden with bags. Kate turned to wave to Jen's father who had brought them both down from York then called out to Gran, announcing her arrival. Sue was never happier than when Kate was home, not that she would have admitted that to her granddaughter. They got on so well together and had the same crazy sense of humour. But Kate was growing up and would soon be making her own way in life.

Sue's thoughts went back to this ramshackle little stone-built cottage. From the old papers she had once found in the dresser drawer, she had been able to piece together its history. It had been built in the mid-1800s to house the head gardener for Skelthorpe Hall. Various names were noted down in the tenancy deeds, and sheets showing rents paid. When Herbert Davis and Kate arrived in 1925, it appeared that Herbert was the last gardener to live there. When the lord died leaving no heirs, the estate fell into disrepair and lay abandoned until after the war. However, Herbert's widow had been given the opportunity to purchase it at a nominal cost and had full rights thereafter.

Sue suspected Kate had been a shrewd manager of the household affairs and thus was able to afford it. From the copy of Herbert's will amongst the papers, she could see he had a reasonable amount of savings but Kate must have been able to amass enough to become sole owner. On her death, she left it to her daughter Eliza, but as far as Sue remembered, it was her own mother Maud who eventually came to live there and it was where Sue had been born – in that very upstairs room where Maud herself had been born, her mother told her. And now Sue had made provision that it should pass to her granddaughter, Kate. Of course, it would be up to Kate what she did with it, but Sue hoped it would continue to shelter and give comfort to further generations.

She was interrupted from her reverie by Kate's collapse, fully laden, into the room.

"Hi Gran! I'm ho-ome!" she shouted, gleefully.

"I think I guessed!" laughed Gran. "Get your stuff upstairs and then tell me all your news. I'll put on the kettle – and there's home-made lemon drizzle cake!"

"Gran, you know me so well!" laughed Kate as she headed up the narrow staircase to her room, staggering under the weight of her laptop, rucksack and of course, her precious writing slope tucked under her arm.

*****

Later that evening they sat outside on the little patio area at the back of the cottage, sharing a bottle of wine and watching the sun sink behind the trees that backed on to what was once the grounds of Skelthorpe Hall. It brought back her train of thought from earlier that day and Gran mentioned to Kate about the generations they knew about that had lived here, and those they knew nothing about.

"I love this little cottage," Kate sighed. "It feels more than just coming home. It's like being enveloped in love…"

Gran laughed. "Sounds like the wine's making you a bit dewy-eyed!"

"I've got an early birthday present for you Gran. I know your birthday isn't till next week but I can't wait to give you it," and she dashed upstairs and returned with a slim cardboard box about the size of a book. "Sorry I haven't wrapped it," she apologised.

Gran accepted the box from her with a quizzical smile and took a few seconds to appreciate what it was, then let out a gasp. "Oh Kate! That's wonderful! I had thought about it – you know Sally did hers ages ago and she's found out all sorts."

"I thought you'd appreciate doing your DNA," smiled Kate. "I wonder what'll come from it! "

Immediately Gran's thoughts returned to all those brick-walls and missing fathers on birth certificates. Who knew what she might find out!

"Oh – I'm going to meet up with Jen next week some time," continued Kate, "She's been on at me for ages but she's finally persuaded me to take up wild swimming. We'll start off easy with a calm river, then who knows?"

"Woooo…" Gran shivered involuntarily, then laughed, "A goose just walked over my grave!"

CHAPTER FORTY-EIGHT

1940 Skelthorpe, Near Lincoln

Violet looked at the small alarm clock that sat on the bedside table, ticking remorselessly day and night, measuring the seconds and minutes, hours and days that Kate had lain between life and death. It amazed her that she had clung on so long after her last heart attack, but hang on she did, barely able to speak now or move, other than to weakly nod or blink her eyes in response to questions. At least, Violet thought, she had stopped the incessant babbling about what she had done and her sense of loathing, the guilt finally causing her to silently weep. Of course, it was all just nonsense. The ravings of someone whose mind had been irreparably damaged by the seizures. Violet tried to calm her, in the end finding that just agreeing with her was the best way to placate her.

She crossed the room and leant over the writing slope box which sat on the dressing table by the window. It had a lacy doily draped over it and Kate would never let anyone open it, even when as children they were intrigued to see what was inside. She pulled open the heavy blackout curtains and let the weak morning light pervade the stuffy room where her step-grandmother lay. An hour had passed since she had slipped silently away from this life. The doctor had come and pronounced her dead and said he would inform the undertaker. Violet turned and looked at the slight form in the bed in front of her. She would go to the village and phone her father and stepmother Lizzie and let them know that the time had come. Poor little Maud, Kate's daughter – now she had no blood family left. She had just turned fifteen and had left school and was learning shorthand and typing, hoping to get a job in the Civil

Service in the future – a secure job, their father assured her. As for herself, she had decided to join the WAAF, only biding her time until Kate needed her care no longer. There were plenty of local chaps joining up and training for the RAF, soon to be posted to one of the airbases around Lincolnshire. She and her twin sister Alice had decided that would go together and join up. As for her younger brother George, he was obsessed with the planes that regularly flew over, learning the types and wishing he was old enough to join them, but he was still just a kid of fourteen.

With a sigh, she took a last look at the old lady that she had looked after for the last year or so and went to pull the sheet over her face. With a start she realised that her eyes were still open, though she had thought that the doctor had closed them. Such pale eyes, grey irises almost colourless with a dark rim around them. There were times when Violet had found their gaze quite unnerving but she wasn't sure that she could close them now. No – she would just leave them and with a sigh, she pulled the linen sheet over them and quietly left the room.

Violet closed the cottage door, shut the gate behind her and headed down the lane to the village. Upstairs the merest puff of air stirred the curtains, the clock stopped ticking and all was still...

***** The End *****

AUTHOR'S NOTE

While standing on the banks of the river Ouse at Naburn, just south of York, I was amazed to find a scattering of seashells washed up on the bank of the river. How could seashells be here, nearly thirty miles from the sea? After speaking to the local lock keepers I discovered that the Ouse is tidal up to that point, where the weir effectively blocks any further wash upstream. Eggs of marine seashells, and the shells themselves, can be carried upstream on the strong high tides, which explains their presence there. And why young Kate was able to pick one up as a memento and put it in her pocket on that fateful night when her mother and brother drowned...

ACKNOWLEDGEMENTS

My thanks go to the enumerable people who have researched, transcribed, digitised and added data to the many family history sites and archives over the years. Without them, today's family historians would have a far harder job. I am especially indebted to those who made the military records accessible and from which I wove Amos' story.

I must also acknowledge the help and support given from 'The Friends of York Cemetery' and in particular Dennis Shaw who supplied much valuable background knowledge and history of the cemetery and burials. Also of interest is the self-guided trail 'Public & Second Class Graves'. This and more information can be found at https://yorkcemeterygenealogy.org.uk

A wealth of websites helped with background information about the history of writing slopes, so much so that I became hooked and ended up by buying an antique one!

Madame Clapham actually existed and Hull Museums Collections website gave much information about this formidable lady.

Thanks also go to my husband's late father and grandfather whose Yorkshire dialect echoed in my ears as I worked on the dialogue. For the purpose of ease of understanding, I made the decision not to use many stand-alone dialect words which might confuse non-British, even non-Yorkshire readers! I have tried to keep the dialogue as understandable as possible whilst acknowledging how working class people would have spoken in those times.

And finally thanks go to my husband for allowing me to take such liberties with his family. Thankfully none of it is true - but the places and events I discovered whilst doing his family research gave me the inspiration for this, the sequel to my first telling of this fanciful tale.

BOOKS BY THIS AUTHOR

Always The River

When Kate heads off to university in York, she is unaware that her grandmother Sue's new-found hobby of family research will unearth a force which will bind her to that place, but in another time as the malevolent spirit of the river threatens to reach out into the present.

As succeeding generations are uncovered by Sue's research, Kate experiences the mysterious hold the river has had over her family while the reader encounters the chilling story of Laura, Kate's four times great-grandmother, who finds herself cast out by her family and having to exist hand to mouth. She is haunted by a voice which both befriends her and makes demands upon her.

Can Laura's determination and strength of will overcome what the river has in store for her and her family?

Will Kate ever truly know the full story of Laura and her tragic past six generations earlier?

In this this darkly sinister and chilling mystery set in both 19th century and present-day Yorkshire, we are witness to the struggles and tragedies that were daily events for the people who worked on and by the rivers and canals. As the story unfolds, the events of the past are revealed as the terrible truth is uncovered.

Set on and by the River Ouse and adjoining waterways, this family saga is woven around actual historical events and family research.

This book is continued in the sequel 'The River Looks After Its Own'.

Prussian Blue

There are stories each generation can tell, but if the next generation isn't listening, they will be lost. Sometimes you realise you are the last link in that chain, and it is up to you to preserve them. So that is what I aimed to do. Taking the lives of three of my extraordinary ancestors – the apothecary, the surgeon and man-midwife and the sea captain, I have woven a narrative around the people, places and events that I have discovered travelling from 1809 in Prussia to the end of that century in N. Ireland.

Discovering the innovative medical training which was being developed in Berlin in the 1840s and learning how that translated to the practice of a small-town medic in Pomerania, was both revealing and addictive, especially when I had access to my ancestor's handwritten archive material from that time. A distinguished surgeon and the first man-midwife in that area, he should have had an illustrious career, but that was tragically cut short. He left behind a young family and I followed his son who broke away and sailed the seas, eventually settling in N. Ireland. Discovering his notorious exploits were also a surprise. Handing over a box full of documents, files and folders left in my will to a distant cousin, who may or may not be interested in the family history, is not a guarantee of its perpetuity. Who is going to plod through all the research and notes I have made? So in order to ensure the information has a chance of being passed on and assimilated, I have constructed this story around the basic facts. I hope that readers, as well as my relatives, will enjoy finding out about my extraordinary ancestors as much as I did.

Through Ice And Fire

On the Russian Arctic convoys in 1942, Leonard H. Thomas kept a secret notebook from which he later wrote his memoirs. These contained many well-observed details of life onboard his ship, HMS Ulster Queen. He detailed observations of the hardships that followed when they endured being at action stations and locked in the engine room, under fire from the skies above and the sea below, and only able to guess at what was happening from the cacophony of sounds they could hear. Thomas tells of how the crew suffered from an appalling lack of food, the intense cold, and the stark conditions endured for weeks on end berthed in Archangel in the cold of the approaching Russian winter. There are also insights about the morale of the men and lighter moments when their humour kept them going. These stories can now be told as his daughter has edited them into an account that illustrates the fortitude and bravery of the men who sailed through ice and fire to further the war effort so far from home.

Printed in Great Britain
by Amazon